Janet Tashjian

Sticker Girl

with illustrations by
INGA WILMINK

SQUARE
FISH

Christy Ottaviano Books

Henry Holt and Company ★ New York

for my nieces

SQUARE FISH

An imprint of Macmillan Publishing Group, LLC
175 Fifth Avenue, New York, NY 10010
mackids.com

Our books may be purchased in bulk for promotional, educational, or business
use. Please contact your local bookseller or the Macmillan Corporate and
Premium Sales Department at (800) 221-7945 ext. 5442 or by
e-mail at MacmillanSpecialMarkets@macmillan.com.

Library of Congress Cataloging-in-Publication Data
Names: Tashjian, Janet, author. | Wilmink, Inga, illustrator.
Title: Sticker girl / Janet Tashjian ; illustrated by Inga Wilmink.
Description: New York : Henry Holt and Company, 2016.
Identifiers: LCCN 2015049897 (print) | LCCN 2016019793 (ebook) |
ISBN 978-1-250-12954-3 (paperback) | ISBN 978-1-62779-338-4 (ebook)
Subjects: | CYAC: Self-confidence–Fiction. | Imagination–Fiction. |
Stickers–Fiction. | Magic–Fiction. | BISAC: JUVENILE FICTION /
Fantasy & Magic. | JUVENILE FICTION / Humorous Stories. |
JUVENILE FICTION / Imagination & Play. | JUVENILE FICTION /
Social Issues / Self-Esteem & Self-Reliance.
Classification: LCC PZ7.T211135 St 2016 (print) |
LCC PZ7.T211135 (ebook) | DDC [Fic]–dc23
LC record available at https://lccn.loc.gov/2015049897

Originally published in the United States by
Christy Ottaviano Books/Henry Holt and Company
First Square Fish edition, 2017
Book designed by April Ward
Square Fish logo designed by Filomena Tuosto

1   3   5   7   9   10   8   6   4   2

AR: 4.6 / LEXILE: 740L

A Little About me

Here's the thing about being shy: just because you're not bowling people over with your giant personality, they might think there's not a lot going on inside.

But they'd be wrong.

Quiet types have rich inner worlds—we just don't let everyone see them. At least that's how my mother explains my shyness to her friends when she thinks I'm not listening. (I usually am.)

Kids in my class may think there's no reason to sit with me at lunch or hang out during recess

because I have nothing to add to their conversations about the latest app or a favorite band. They don't understand that I know every word to the newest songs, that I kill at Candy Crush, or that I've memorized chunks of dialogue from most Disney movies. No one would guess I'm a good singer like my mom or that I make up crazy stories like my abuelita.

My inner world is exciting and fun.

My outer world?

Not so much.

What I
Love Most

I live with my family in the San Fernando Valley, north of Los Angeles. I'm the middle child, sandwiched between my older brother, Eric, and my younger brother, James. Their boy energy pretty much sucks the life out of the house, so I spend a lot of time in my room by myself.

Being alone is great once you get used to it, although I wouldn't mind having a best friend one of these days. I'm giving it some time since we moved here from San Diego last year. It's coming up on my twelve-month deadline soon, but I'm not worried. Yet.

I have a great imagination—sometimes I pretend my Chihuahua, Lily, is an injured soldier I have to save on the battlefield. Sometimes I make short videos of her talking in an Italian accent. My abuelita tells me I need to make more of an effort to find new friends who aren't Chihuahuas. I tell her I am happy to entertain myself, that I like keeping busy.

And my favorite way to keep busy is playing with stickers.

I don't just like stickers . . .

I LOVE stickers!

Animal stickers, ballerina stickers, dragon stickers, voice bubble stickers—I have thousands of them.

I put stickers on notebooks, on clothes, on my bureau and my mirror and the shelves in my room. I put them on my mom's computer; I put them on my dad's bowling ball and my abuelita's gardening tools.

You could say that stickers keep me company when Eric is blasting music with his friends or

James is dumping a box of cereal down the toilet. In the world of stickers, I'M the one in charge. Stickers don't judge you; they don't care if you're quiet or shy. My stickers keep me company while I'm eating lunch by myself at school.

I'm not sure where my life would be without them.

Presents!

When Dad comes back from the restaurant convention, he has presents for all of us. Yay!

My dad has a beard and is kind of short; my brother Eric is already two inches taller. Dad's metabolism is fast, which is good because he needs a lot of energy to run his diner. Buying the diner was the reason we moved here from San Diego. My parents insist it's a great opportunity; they're probably right, but so far it has just been a lot of work.

Dad gives Eric a new case for his phone—his old one is worn, so you can barely see the Kings

logo. Eric is fifteen, and I'm still not used to his skimpy new mustache. It's weird to see hair on the face of someone who drinks milk from the carton and whose feet smell like a moldy cheese factory.

James's eyes light up when Dad hands him a bright red plastic toolbox. James has mischievous eyes that always look like he's about to run into the street. He laughs a lot and has my father's turbo energy. He can crawl faster than any land mammal recorded in *The Guinness Book of World Records*.

I don't have to ask what Dad brought back for me—he gets me the same thing every time he goes away: a new sheet of stickers.

"It was strange," Dad says. "I stopped at this roadside store on a back road near Pomona. This old woman with long gray hair gave me directions to the highway. She had a tattoo of a peacock on her hand and a mysterious smile. She handed me this sheet of stickers and said, 'Your daughter will love these.'"

"How did she know you had a daughter?"

Dad holds up his phone with the screenshot of all of us at the beach. "I guess she noticed my phone when I was picking out James's toolbox. She wouldn't let me pay for either of them."

FREE stickers and toys? Even better. The stickers are faded, as if they've been sitting in the store window for years.

Mom comes in with an armload of groceries. "William, you spoil these kids!"

It's a running joke between them—anyone looking inside our house with its second-hand furniture and homemade curtains would know we're hardly spoiled. But there's no one better than my mom at stretching two paychecks as far as possible. Some people might say Mom is cheap, but I've always looked at her as creative. Not everyone can weave together plastic strawberry baskets into a sturdy end table or upholster dining room chairs with burlap from bags of rice. Sometimes she goes too far—disassembling James's toys to save the life of

the batteries—but most of the time I'm in awe of her imagination.

A lot of other moms wear their shirts untucked or wear yoga pants in the pickup line at school, but my mom always wears a freshly ironed shirt tucked into a nice pair of "slacks." (Her word, not mine.) Both my parents speak fluent Spanish, but Mom also speaks Portuguese because the insurance company she's worked at for years is based in Brazil. Even when she's overworked, Mom rarely gets angry or impatient. My father's personality is more fiery, like my abuelita. Mom is super organized. People say I take after her, and I guess I do.

"And this is for you, mi amor." My father hands Mom a box of individually wrapped dark chocolates. She knows he probably got them as a giveaway at the restaurant convention, but she loves chocolate and loves my

dad, so she kisses him and makes a fuss over how fantastic they are.

I help Mom unpack the groceries until she shoos me away to do my homework.

But homework is the last thing on my mind.

I have new stickers!

what?!

It takes several minutes to decide which sticker to use first. I finally choose the rainbow to put on my keychain. (Rainbow is my favorite color!)

But something about this sheet feels different. As soon as I start peeling, the sticker begins to rumble. There's a *swooshing* sound, and a puff of confetti explodes from the sticker sheet.

whoosh! POOF! BAM!

WHAT IS HAPPENING?

The sticker transforms into a

rainbow.

(Yes—the sticker becomes *real*, in the middle of my room.)

I stare at the multicolored arch spanning from the window to the door, then let out a bloodcurdling scream. "DAD! A rainbow!"

"That's funny—it wasn't supposed to rain."

My dad comes down the hall, sorting through the mail without looking up.

"THE RAINBOW STICKER IS REAL!"

"I thought the images were lifelike too."

I gaze at the blue, green, and yellow stripes covering my room. "Dad, LOOK!"

My father picks up his ringing cell and goes to the kitchen to take the call.

I suddenly wonder if *other* stickers will come to life now too. I pull out my roll of horse stickers, my sheets of farmyard animals and candy stickers. *Is there going to be a horse in my room?* Because that would be AWESOME! But the horses, barns, and jelly beans lie limp in my hands after I peel them. I open my eyes wide. The rainbow still glistens over my bed.

The next sticker on the new sheet is a skateboard.

I remove it from the backing, slowly. Gently.

whoosh! Poof! Bam!

I clench my eyes, almost afraid.

 14

As soon as the sticker leaves the page, it trans-forms into a real

skateboard

in my hands.

THIS IS INSANE!

"MOM!!!"

My mother runs into the room chasing my brother James, who carries an armload of her shoes. "Martina, stop screaming. You're scaring your brother." James is drooling on the rug and throwing shoes; he doesn't seem too scared to me.

Mom glances at the skateboard in my hands. "I'm so glad you're going to get some exercise!

Make sure you wear a helmet and pads." My brother drops the shoes and tries to grab the skateboard.

"Mom, this skateboard was a sticker—it just came to life!"

She barely pays attention as she wipes my brother's chin. "Lots of people decorate skateboards with stickers, and given how much you love them, I wouldn't expect anything else." She's so busy trying to grab James that she doesn't notice she's standing underneath a rainbow.

Mom races down the hall after my brother and I realize my parents are never going to believe I have magical stickers. It looks like I'll be keeping the power of these amazing stickers to myself—which is perfectly fine with me.

my new Best Friends

I'm as thrifty as my mom, so nothing makes me feel worse than waste. And with only eight magic stickers left on the sheet, I have to use each one CAREFULLY.

It takes me a while to fade the rainbow so my parents don't discover it. I finally succeed with my hair dryer. (Thank you, last year's science fair!)

I kick off my sneakers and jump on my bed to examine the rest of the stickers.

♥ cupcake with a smiling face

♥ pitcher
of punch

♥ fairy

♥ polka-
dot dress

♥ Pegasus

♥ key

♥ ladybug with a karaoke machine

♥ three puppies wearing party hats

These stickers look like they're just *itching* for me to peel them off.

But I can't.

I wrap the sheet inside several tissues, then slip it into a gift bag and hide it in an empty shoebox in my closet. I need to savor the stickers, make them last—at least until I get Dad to take me back to that store with the mysterious old lady.

I'm too excited to do homework, so I make sure Eric's not home before sneaking into the garage to grab my bike helmet and his knee pads. I've only skateboarded a few times and never successfully. But this is my *own* skateboard, so I'll have lots of time to practice.

I make sure no cars are coming, then jump on.

The craziest part isn't that I'm riding on a skateboard that used to be a sticker. The crazy part is, I'm *good*. I skate around the parked cars, down the hill, and expertly turn at the bottom of the street.

A guy wearing earbuds walking his dog gives me a thumbs-up as I whiz by.

I can skateboard!

I have magic stickers!

I have a PEGASUS!!

I'm a nine-year-old with superpowers!

I am magic! I am special!

I am Sticker Girl!

Even sticker girl can have a Bad Day

I suppose some kids couldn't wait to bring magical stickers into show-and-tell, but not me—I'm definitely going to keep my secret identity hidden. The last thing I want to do is attract attention and having supernatural stickers doesn't change that one bit.

On the bus, I open my pack several times to make sure my stickers are safe. (Of COURSE I decided to bring them to school—wouldn't you?) Even with magic in my backpack, I still sit by myself and observe the other kids as if it's just a regular day.

It's not like I'm trying to eavesdrop on my classmate Bev as we ride, but she talks with so much energy, it's difficult not to listen. She entertains two rows of kids with a story about a skunk trapped in her garage. It's hard not to laugh when she acts out her panic-stricken mother, the frightened skunk, and her father running around the yard after being sprayed. I almost want to applaud when she's finished, not just because the story's funny but because Bev is so confident. I'd give anything to be like that in the world.

I've never talked to Bev, but she seems nice. She's taller than I am, which maybe accounts for all that confidence. Her hair's blond and long, but the back of it never seems brushed as if she's got a million more important things to do in the morning. And she *totally* exaggerates. Once I heard her make up a story about one of the most popular boys in our class—Mike Belmont— knocking her over in the hall. I was there when it happened—he barely grazed her—but the story made it sound like the opening scene of a funny new reality show. If my inner world is exciting like Mom says, Bev's *outer* world is.

At school, Ms. Graham starts by talking about things going on in the news. Ms. Graham has the deepest dimples I've ever seen, on both cheeks. Her hair is salt-and-pepper gray, but sometimes she gets it highlighted. This week it's black and white and kind of orange too.

"There's some national news happening in Los Angeles this week—does anybody know what it is?" she asks.

I'm sure she's talking about the Olympic try-outs, but I don't raise my hand. In fact, I've never raised my hand in Ms. Graham's or any teacher's class since I've been at this school.

"Somebody must know," Ms. Graham continues. "There are signs up everywhere."

Even though Tommy and Lisa are now waving their arms in the air, Ms. Graham zeroes in on me. "Any ideas, Martina?"

I've been wondering how long it will take for Ms. Graham to figure out that I know the answers to a lot of her questions but don't have the courage to speak in front of the class. I smile and shrug as if I don't have a clue.

Ms. Graham continues to ignore Tommy and Lisa and returns my smile. "How about if I give you a hint?"

I don't need a hint. I need you to call on someone else! I feel my cheeks burn, and when I look around the room, several of my classmates are staring.

Ms. Graham looks at me with kindness and tells me to take my time.

I know she spoke to my mother last month about me "coming out of my shell," but why do I have to do it *now*? I've done a good job of keeping a low profile, and I'd like it to stay that way. When I look around at my classmates' faces, I realize if I don't answer, they might think I'm a dope.

The Olympic tryouts, I want to say. *Athletes from all over the world are here.*

But I don't say that. I doodle in my notebook, not meeting my teacher's eyes.

Ms. Graham nods, then calls on Tommy.

"Olympic tryouts!" Tommy answers.

I focus on my paper as if I'm writing the most important sentence in the world. What if my answer was wrong? What if someone made a joke? Without looking up, I glance to the next row, where Lisa and Bev are still looking at me. Their expressions aren't mean, just curious. They probably wonder  why I can't answer the simplest of questions. They probably wonder what I'm afraid of.

I wonder about those things too.

The Day gets worse

We're doing a dinosaur project this afternoon and I pray we don't have to work in pairs; I always get more done when I don't have the stress of talking to a classmate. But the day continues to go downhill when Ms. Graham hands out assignments. Last time, she paired me with Tommy, who told jokes while I did all the work.

Ms. Graham shoots me a little smile as if she's presenting me with a gift. "Martina and Bev, you're together on this."

Pairing me with the most popular girl in our

class isn't going to make me more talkative. Even with magic stickers tucked into my bag, this is the worst school day ever.

Bev waits at her desk, so I drag my chair over. I take out my notebook and pen, ready to write down anything she has to say.

"I don't know much about dinosaurs." Bev speaks so loudly, Lisa three seats over yells out, "Neither do I!"

I rummage through my pack and take out a roll of dinosaur stickers I got for my birthday. (Yes, I always carry several packs of stickers with me. How else would I get through lunch and recess?)

Bev scans the roll and points to the pterodactyl. "That one's cute."

Technically pterodactyls aren't dinosaurs—they're pterosaurs—but I don't have the nerve to correct her.

"Well, are we going to do this or what?"

I peel a pterodactyl and stick it on a blank page in my notebook. Bev spots the rest of the stickers peeking out of my pack. "Hey, can I have that one?" She motions to the happy cupcake on my magic sheet.

Sharing is something I'm actually good at and sharing with someone fun like Bev would be a real step forward in the friendship department. But suppose the cupcake comes to life in the middle of class?

"We should probably get to work," I finally say.

"So you *can* talk!" Bev says. "We all thought you just played with stickers."

My classmates *have* talked about me—my worst nightmare.

Bev points to my bag again. "How about that cupcake?"

I can't believe she's not letting this go. "I'm sorry, I can't give you that one," I say softly.

Bev points to the many sheets of stickers in my pack. "You have tons!" she says. "What's one lousy sticker?"

I peel off a triceratops and hand it to her. Bev looks at me closely, and I can almost see her deciding that I'm not worth the effort of getting to know. After a moment, she gets up and switches places with Tommy so she can sit with Lisa to do the report.

"Knock-knock," Tommy says, slipping into the desk beside me.

"Who's there?" I answer quietly.

"Avenue."

"Avenue who?"

"Avenue heard this joke before?" Tommy elbows me as if it's the funniest joke on the planet. But I'm looking over at Bev and Lisa laughing and hoping it isn't about me.

A Snotty Pastry

On the bus ride home, I think of all the witty things I could've talked to Bev about. Why didn't I mention the great coconut cupcakes my abuelita makes or that place in Beverly Hills with the cupcake ATM? There's a lot I can share about cupcakes—just not that sticker. These magic stickers are starting to feel more like magic *problems*.

When I get home, I close my door and take out the sheet of stickers. I agree with Bev—the cupcake with the smiling face *does* look good. I head to the kitchen to grab some peanut butter cookies so I don't get tempted to eat the cupcake once it comes to life.

I slowly peel the cupcake off the page.

whoosh! Poof! Bam!

The cUPcaKe

practically jumps out of my hand. Lily runs around in circles and barks.

"Thank you so much!" the cupcake says. "I was starting to get stale."

"You TALK?"

"I have a mouth, don't I? And eyes? I can do a lot of things." The cupcake breaks into the chorus of "I Want to Hold Your Hand."

"You like the Beatles?"

"Of course I like the Beatles. Who doesn't?"

He sounds a little snippy, but I don't complain. I'm hanging out with a cupcake, after all. I pick him up and place him on my desk until Lily calms down.

"You want to tell me what's going on? I've never had stickers come to life before. Are there any rules I'm supposed to follow? Some order to use the stickers in?"

"How do *I* know? Next thing, you'll be asking if I'm gluten-free."

I'm not sure I like this cupcake's attitude.

"My name's Craig, by the way. What do you do for fun around here?"

"We can watch a video," I suggest. "Want to see a dog get stuck in a revolving door?"

I get the laptop from my brother's room and play the video. Craig chuckles as he watches. He makes me play it three more times, then chooses one of a kitten tumbling out of a laundry basket.

"I've been missing out," Craig says. "Can we do this tomorrow too?"

I tell him I have school.

"I've heard about school. Can I come?"

"You came with me today." The thought of my lame interaction with Bev makes me wince.

"But I wasn't alive yet! I want to participate!"

"Well, you can't be yakking all day—I could get in trouble."

"That doesn't sound like MY problem," Craig says. "What a Goody Two-shoes."

This cupcake is starting to get on my nerves. I tell Craig if he doesn't behave, I might have to eat him.

He looks me in the eye. "Gee, I hope I don't go down the wrong pipe and you end up choking. That would be a shame."

Did I just get threatened by a pastry? "Hey, no one likes a bossy cupcake. Just because you *can* talk, doesn't mean you have to."

"It's bad manners to yell at baked goods—everybody knows that." Bits of frosting fly off him as he speaks.

I'm not sure if these magical stickers are all they're cracked up to be.

mi gran Familia

Every Sunday my cousins, aunts, uncles, my abuelita, and some of her friends get together at the park near our house for a big meal. My dad's usually in charge of food; he often barbecues ribs, or on a special occasion, roasts a pig, but today he gave in to my cousins' requests for hot dogs and hamburgers. It's not that we don't appreciate Dad's carne asada or chiles rellenos, but sometimes there's nothing better than a freshly grilled burger with cheese.

My brother Eric and some of the other cousins skateboard in the parking lot. I've been really careful not to leave my magic skateboard lying around. I'd never see it again if Eric got ahold of it. My cousins Tanya, Paula, and I play our favorite game—waitress. We go to each table and take everyone's orders, yelling requests to my dad. He always cooks whatever he wants anyway but repeats what we order just to play along. Whenever the family gets together at the diner, my cousins and I go booth to booth, pencils tucked behind our ears the way Dad's real waitress, Susanna, does. Dad says when I'm a few years older, I can graduate from filling the sugar caddies to actually getting paid.

My abuelita has the seat of honor at the head of the picnic table in the aluminum folding chair she's had for decades. Mom says my abuelita has a soft spot in her heart for me, but I think she treats all her grandchildren as if they're special.

My abuelita used to live with us in San Diego, but when we moved to the San Fernando Valley, she got her own apartment here too. Our neighbors used to call my abuelita *la bruja*, which means "the witch." She's not a witch, of course,

but that didn't stop them from asking her to tell their fortunes or attend a home birth. To my cousins and me, she's just our grandmother with the colorful clothes and the dangly earrings.

She takes the cane she's used since her hip surgery and hooks my arm. I pretend like she's dragging me, then sit beside her.

"Have you made any new friends at school yet?" she asks.

I tell her about all the fun kids in my class, none of whom can be called friends.

My abuelita sees right through me. "It's hard to make friends, especially when you're shy."

I brace myself for what's coming next.

"You need to try harder, Marti," she says. "You need to make more of an effort."

I'm immune to this pep talk, the same one my mother's given a dozen times. *Why don't you sing at school like you do at home? Why don't you share some of your stories?* Sure, Mom—maybe while Mike Belmont or Bev Swanson holds court after school, I'll sing them the song I made up about the rhinoceros pastry chef. (Swirly frosting comes out of its horn like a nozzle. It's one of my favorites.) My abuelita and Mom mean well, but neither of them understands how hard it is for me.

"Tell me how you're doing," she continues.

If I tell anyone about my magical stickers, it will be my abuelita. I actually practiced saying the words "my stickers come to life" in front of the mirror last night, and it sounded ridiculous.

I tell my grandmother there's nothing special going on, even though I've got a soon-to-be-real Pegasus in my bag.

When Tanya takes out her guitar, I run over to join in. After a few songs, my father makes a big to-do out of the platter of hot dogs and hamburgers, reciting the endless list of condiments to accompany them. As I wait in line, I spot my little brother opening my bag, which is propped against a tree with the others.

"James Edgardo!" I grab my purse from him and check inside to see if Craig is okay.

"Cupcake!" James says.

My mother scoops up my brother. "No dessert until you've eaten lunch, niño!"

James tries to wriggle out of her arms, wildly pointing to my bag. "Cupcake!"

My mom gives me a sly smile. "You and Tanya aren't eating dessert first again, are you?"

I give her a slow smile back. "Maybe . . ."

As she wrangles James to her lap at the picnic table, I open my purse.

"That monster was going to *eat* me!" Craig says. "He's an animal!"

"He's two years old, and you're a cupcake," I answer. "Do the math."

It takes a few minutes to settle down my hysterical cupcake. Then I load my hamburger with chilies and pickles and join Tanya and Paula underneath the tree. It's a fun afternoon joking around with my grandmother, my cousins, my mom, even my grumpy uncle David. So why is it so hard to do the same thing with the kids at school?

I help my abuelita to the parking lot at the end of the afternoon. She's small—not much taller than I am—and bends gracefully into the backseat of my uncle's car. "Do you promise you're going to try a little harder to make friends, Marti?" she asks.

"I promise." I hand her the cane, and she winks through the window as they drive away.

I can feel a rumbling in my purse. Sure enough, it's Craig. "I promise," he mimics.

He's making fun of me, but the crazy thing is, his impersonation is spot on. His voice sounds *exactly* like mine. Even Lily looks up as if I were talking.

Craig seems awfully proud of himself. "I'm very good at impressions. Want to hear my Elmo?"

I actually *do* want to hear his Elmo, but my father honks the horn to let me know they're

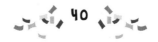

waiting. The whole way home, Eric grabs my flip-flops and pretends to throw them out the window. It's annoying, but I don't get angry. I'm filled with the glow of family and sun and food and not even a stupid older brother can ruin it.

FOOD Fight

James is wearing a colander on his head, which I'm guessing is supposed to be a hard hat, since he's got his toolbox and is sticking the toy screwdriver into every nook and cranny in my room.

He spots Craig on my desk. "Cupcake!"

"It's too close to dinnertime," I say. "Besides this cupcake doesn't taste good."

"Hey!" Craig shouts.

James looks up, eyes alert. "Cupcake talk!"

I shoot Craig a look to keep quiet. "Cupcakes don't talk, James. Come on, let me help you build something with those tools. Look, you've got a hammer! And this toolbox locks!"

"Cupcake talk!"

"See what you did?" I whisper to Craig. "Now my parents are going to wonder what he's talking about."

Craig shakes his head. "You never should've said I didn't taste good. Actually, I'm quite delicious. The sour cream in the batter adds some real tang."

Thankfully, Mom comes in to get James for his appointment with the pediatrician.

"Cupcake talk!" James claps his hands together like this is the best thing ever, which isn't far from the truth.

"I *wish* cupcakes could talk," Mom says. "Doughnuts too."

Craig's about to open his big mouth again, so I shove him into my sock drawer. Mom says she

and James will be back in an hour and to set the table for dinner.

When I open the sock drawer, Craig is not happy. "I could've suffocated!"

I take several pairs of socks and shake them out. "You got crumbs everywhere!"

Lily jumps off the bed and starts sniffing around for a snack.

"Keep that overgrown rat away from me!" Craig shouts.

I pick up Lily and put her in her favorite spot, between my two corduroy pillows. "Dogs can die from eating chocolate—don't you know that? I'd *never* let her eat you!"

"You're more concerned about a mangy dog who doesn't talk than you are about me?"

"First of all, Lily's not mangy. Second, I'm *glad* she doesn't talk if it means complaining all the time. I hope these other stickers aren't as negative as you are."

Craig sulks for a few minutes on my desk before finally coming around. "So what do you want to do?"

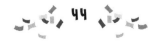

"I was going to play with stickers," I say sheepishly.

He points to the puppies on the magic sheet. "You know you're dying to play with them. What are you waiting for? Peel them off!"

"I'm using regular stickers today." I take out the roll of animal stickers I got in my Easter basket last year.

"I'm not sure I've ever seen anyone play with us before," Craig says. "What do you *do*?"

"Stick them on things."

"Duh!" Craig rolls his eyes.

"Sometimes I make up stories to go along with them." I place the buffalo and horse stickers on a sheet of orange construction paper. I follow those with stickers of a wolf and deer. Grabbing a marker, I draw an arch from one side of the page to the other.

"That looks like a cave painting," Craig says.

His comment makes me happy because that's exactly what I was going for. It's fun having someone in my room to help me play with my sticker collection, even if it *is* a piece of food.

45

"We cupcakes have a lot to contribute, you know. We're not just empty calories."

I'm sure that can be debated, but I get the idea.

Craig looks at me with a smile. "You've got a great imagination."

"Are you trying to butter me up?" I ask. "That's a cupcake joke."

He ignores me. "You're fun—you must have a lot of friends."

The statement takes me by surprise. "I do," I stammer. "Lots."

He nods. "I thought so."

I can't even lie to a cupcake. "Okay, I *don't* have a lot of friends, but it's only because we just moved here last year."

"Last year isn't 'just moved.' Did you have friends at your other school?"

"Of course I did." I tell Craig about my best friend, Denise, who lived next door.

I expect him to say something snotty, but instead he seems sincere. "Sometimes one good friend is all you need."

I return the smile. Denise *was* a good friend; we've talked a few times on the phone, but I've only seen her once since we moved. We used to play with stickers all the time. If she ever knew I had magical stickers, she'd make me use all of them immediately.

I point to the magic sheet. "Is there some kind of time limit, or are you guys here forever?"

"It's not like I have an instruction manual," Craig answers. "But I think we *do* go back."

I feel the floor release underneath me. "What do you *mean*?"

Craig shrugs. "I don't remember how or when. . . . Maybe it has something to do with the weather."

"The *weather?*"

"Or maybe there's a certain date? I forget."

"You have to go back, but you forget when?!"

"Hey, I'm doing the best I can here! Sheesh!"

"I need to know the rules if I'm going to be Sticker Girl," I complain. "Think!"

"**You're not the boss,**"

Craig yells.

"**We don't work for you!**"

He turns his back and pretends to examine my bedspread.

I head to the kitchen to set the table. It's too bad chocolate is deadly for dogs, because I kind of want to feed Craig to Lily right now.

My Cupcake is a Ventriloquist

Ms. Graham waves a piece of paper in front of the class. "It's time for our end-of-the-year projects where you get to focus on one of the many exciting subjects you learned this year."

No one seems anywhere near as thrilled as Ms. Graham is.

"For the next few weeks, you're going to work in teams of three and perform a presentation or skit about one of the topics on this list."

Did she just say *perform*? *In teams of three?*

My mind immediately goes back to the

kickball tournament a few months ago in PE. Not only was I picked last out of three classes, I flubbed the final point and my team lost. I'm actually pretty good at kickball, but what I'm *not* good at is performing.

Ms. Graham looks straight at me. "Who would you like to work with, Martina?"

For someone like me, being picked first is almost as bad as being picked last. Who am I supposed to pick? I've hardly spoken to anyone all year!

Maybe Ms. Graham will see the burn sweeping across my cheeks and move on to someone else.

She doesn't.

The entire class waits.

I feel a stirring in my bag, which is looped across the back of my chair. "I'll work with Bev and Mike."

Everyone in the class turns around. But it wasn't me who volunteered; it was Craig, doing a perfect impersonation of my voice.

"What a nice choice." She motions for Bev and Mike to bring their chairs to my desk. My cupcake sticker just volunteered me to create a project with the two most popular kids in class. Ms. Graham looks a bit bewildered; so does everyone else.

Bev and Mike shoot each other a look as if to say, *How do we get out of this?*

I don't blame them because I'm asking the same question.

Mike pulls his chair alongside mine. He's wearing striped surf shorts and a T-shirt with a cartoon werewolf. He plays soccer in the town league and has blond curly hair. He's never spoken to me before.

Bev passes out the pages from Ms. Graham. "So, we meet again. We might as well decide on a topic."

I pretend to study the list of subjects, hoping Bev or Mike will decide so I won't have to.

"We can do the Incas," Mike suggests. "Or the food chain."

Bev nods. "I like maps too."

I almost jump out of my seat when I hear Craig's voice, perfectly imitating mine. "How about the first one? I'm an *expert* on that."

My eyes race to the top of the list.

"You're an expert on constellations?" Bev asks.

I duck behind the paper in case Craig tries to talk for me again, which of course he does.

"You should've seen the project I did at my last school!"

Mike tosses the paper across the desk. "The easier, the better," he says. "Constellations sound good to me."

Bev eyes me suspiciously, then begins to speak. Luckily for me, so does Ms. Graham. "I can already tell these projects are going to be great! We'll start on them first thing tomorrow."

I wait until everyone files out of the class and

grab my bag. Craig looks very smug, settled in next to my keys.

"Why did you *do* that?" I whisper-shout. "I don't know *anything* about constellations—never mind working on a project with Bev and Mike!"

Craig jumps out of my bag and onto my desk. "You promised your grandmother you'd try to make new friends. And last night you admitted you weren't having any luck. Volunteering to work with Bev and Mike is a step in the right direction."

"How do you even know their names?"

"Cupcakes are smart," Craig answers. "When are you going to get that through your head?"

I hear a noise behind me and stop talking. Bev strolls back into the room and grabs a folder from her desk. She looks at Craig, now standing perfectly still.

"Hey, didn't you have a sticker like that the other day? Same swirly frosting? Same little eyes and mouth?"

Craig had better not blow this. He's caused

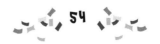

enough trouble for one day. I mumble something about the cupcake maybe looking like one of my stickers.

"Can I see that sheet of stickers again?" Bev asks. "You had some puppies too, right? And a Pegasus? I have a great visual memory."

The magical stickers are in my bag, but I can't let Bev see that Craig is off the sheet.

"Uhm, I'm late for math." I pick up Craig and place him in my bag.

Bev blocks my path. "I'm kind of hungry—want to split that cupcake?"

It sounds as if Craig just gasped. I pray Bev didn't hear him.

I lie and tell her I'm still full from lunch. All I want is to roll up like an armadillo and hide underneath my desk.

She looks at me then at Craig. Then back to me. "I can't wait to hear all your fun facts about constellations."

I can't tell if she's being sarcastic or friendly.

It's a terrible day to be Sticker Girl.

NOOOOOOOO!!!

My parents are excited I'll be collaborating on a year-end project with two kids from my class. I leave out the part of the story where I was pushed into the whole thing by a cupcake.

She and my dad are folding clothes on the kitchen table while my abuelita stirs her famous chicken stew at the stove.

"You kids can work in the diner one afternoon if you want," Dad suggests. "Have some shakes and fries to keep up your energy."

I tell him that sounds great, knowing I'll never have the nerve to invite Bev and Mike. I may be working on a project with the most popular kids in school, but I sure feel pretty alone. And there's only one thing to do when you feel lonely . . .

and that's play with stickers.

I haven't used my magic sheet since I peeled off Craig and what a mistake *that* was. (Although I do love riding my skateboard when Eric's not home. He would *totally* steal it.) I've given a lot of thought to watching a Pegasus come to life before my eyes. Since it's a mythological animal, no one in history has ever seen one. I—Martina Rivera— will be the FIRST PERSON ON THE PLANET

to see a Pegasus, not to mention have one as a pet. (Oh yeah, I'm *keeping* her. I'm not sure if the Pegasus is male or female, but it's pink so I'm calling her Evelyn until I find out otherwise.) I already know I'm going to love Evelyn forever.

Because I'm organized, I've prepared for Evelyn's arrival by storing up grass clippings and carrots in the garage. I have no idea what a Pegasus eats but until I know what Evelyn likes, I figure this is a good start.

Of course there are a few downsides to having a Pegasus. Number one: it could fly away. Which is why I've gone to such lengths to make everything perfect for Evelyn right here in our backyard and have a long piece of rope attached to the fence to make sure she at least stays for a while.

Problem number two: my parents. Having a living, breathing mythological creature in the backyard is not something I'm going to be able to hide for long, so I'm prepared to tell them everything about my magical stickers. Keeping a secret is one thing, but a real-life Pegasus in the back-yard is something else altogether.

I make sure the gate is locked, then put Lily in the house so she won't frighten Evelyn. But what I find when I come back outside makes me shriek in horror.

"JAMES EDGARDO! What are you doing?!"

I race toward the fence, where my brother is holding the magical sheet of stickers, which means he's been in my room again. I think better of it and slow down, trying the calm voice my mother uses when James is about to do something dangerous like jump off the hood of a car.

"James? You need to put that down NOW."

My little brother looks up at me with his big dark eyes. "Horsey."

I take a few more steps toward him. "How about if I give you your own roll of horsey stickers? Stickers you can KEEP."

James's hand hovers over the Pegasus. And before I can yell "NO!!" he's peeled off the sticker.

whoosh! poof! Bam!

The Pegasus

flies off the paper and into the yard. She's a deep pink and her wingspan is at least twelve feet across. Her eyes are blue and her mane is soft and fluffy like cotton candy.

"Horsey!" James squeals. "Pink horsey!"

"Hello, Evelyn," I coo. "My name's Martina."

Evelyn nuzzles her nose against my cheek. Her breath is warm and smells like peppermint.

"We're going to have so many amazing adventures," I tell her. "We can fly through the clouds and across the rooftops. It'll be great!"

The Pegasus leans against me and sighs. It's the most perfect moment of my life.

I reach over to pet this beautiful creature, who suddenly rears up on her hind legs.

And flies away.

"NOOOOOOOOO!" I scream.

"come back!"

I watch the Pegasus soar over the garage.

"We can go to SeaWorld!" I shout. "Have a tea party! Go to the beach! Watch TV! Just STAY!"

Evelyn disappears into the clouds.

"Horsey fly away." James reaches for the next sticker, a key.

"Give me that!" I knew my parents never should've had another kid. I knew it from the moment they told me I was going to have a little brother. I grab the sheet of stickers from James before he wastes any more of my magic.

My abuelita comes outside with a basket of laundry. "What's all the commotion? I could hear you from the laundry room."

"JAMES IS THE WORST BROTHER IN THE HISTORY OF THE WORLD!" I yell.

"Oh, Marti—don't be so dramatic."

"Pink horsey go bye-bye."

As I go inside and slam the door, my two-year-old brother continues to wave to the empty sky.

A Bright Idea

If there's one thing almost as bad as losing a Pegasus, it's working with two talkative class-mates on a subject you know absolutely nothing about. I scoured my notes last night to find what I wrote when we studied constellations earlier in the year, but it was right before the holidays and I was so excited I barely wrote down anything. So I borrow my brother's laptop to find some information online to prepare to be the group's "expert."

Some basic facts:

- There are eighty-eight constellations.

- Constellations appear in both hemispheres.

- The sun is the most famous star but is not in a constellation.

The facts are interesting but don't spark an idea for a project. It's just a matter of time before my classmates realize I'm a fraud. What am I going to do? I pull out my sheet of magical stickers. Maybe the fairy can grant me a wish and make me an overnight expert on constellations.

"I'm surprised you waited this long to use the fairy," Craig says. "Most girls use that one first."

I scroll through my playlist to find an appropriate song for releasing a fairy into the world and settle on one from *Aladdin*.

I slowly peel the sticker from the sheet.

whoosh! poof! Bam!

The fairy

is adorable, the size of my finger. As soon as she appears, she doesn't fly or grant a wish or sparkle.

She yawns.

"You woke me up!" The fairy rubs her eyes. "What *time* is it?"

I tell her it's almost four o'clock, plenty of time for us to do lots of cool stuff together. (I don't tell her I'd originally planned to do these fun activities with the Pegasus.)

"I love to nap," she confesses. "I need a good twelve hours of sleep or I'm a mess."

"Well, maybe we can go outside and play," I suggest.

"Okay, but I have to warn you—I get bored easily."

This fairy's attitude seems worse than Craig's. She finally rouses herself awake and flies around my head.

I sniff the air and tell her something smells like potato chips.

"It's probably me," she says. "I had a snack before my nap. I *love* potato chips. And licorice. And cereal. And popcorn. And Twinkies."

Out of the corner of my eye, I watch Craig hide behind the lamp on my nightstand.

As she continues to fly around, the fairy introduces herself as Lucinda. "How about if I braid your hair? I'm really good at braiding."

I tell her I would *love* that.

"I will *absolutely* braid your hair tomorrow. But right now I'm so tired."

"You just woke up!"

The fairy lands on my pillow and promptly falls asleep.

"Well, *she's* a barrel of laughs," Craig says. "A

sleepy fairy who loves to eat—keep her away from me."

I hate to agree, but I'm disappointed with Lucinda too.

"The last fairy sticker I knew was a hundred times more fun," Craig says. "You got a raw deal with this one." A chunk of Craig's frosting drops to the floor. "Hey! I thought you were going to keep me from falling apart!"

I point to the sleeping fairy. "Maybe she has some magical powers that can keep you from crumbling."

We both watch Lucinda sleep. She rolls over and starts snoring. A loud snort that goes on for several minutes.

"I'll just get a plastic container from the kitchen," I suggest.

The bottom drawer in the kitchen that holds all the containers is always a mess so it takes me a while to find a cover that matches the correct dish. I place Craig gently in the container, hoping he won't lose any more crumbs. I snap the cover in place.

"Hey!" he shouts. "It's stuffy in here!"

"You complain about crumbling. You complain about staying fresh—make up your mind!"

The fairy stretches, then rolls over. "Can you guys keep it down? I'm trying to sleep."

I look at the back of the little fairy's head. I look at Craig, pouting inside his plastic dish. I stare at the rest of the stickers on the sheet: dress, puppies, ladybug, pitcher, key.

Which of these stickers can help me with my school project?

A SOGGY MESS

We're making abstract paintings in Mrs. Larussa's class. As soon as I see Tommy and Billy wrestling in the back of the room, I gather my paints close. Tommy's like a puppy that hasn't been house-trained, jumping on furniture and knocking things over everywhere he goes.

It seems as if I'm the only one worried—even Mrs. Larussa isn't paying attention to their monkey business in the back of the room. It's one of the benefits of being shy; you spend so much time observing, you become an expert on every kid in your class.

Sure enough, Tommy rams himself into one of the benches, knocking over several open jars. Bev jumps up from her seat, her jeans now covered in giant splashes of dark red paint. Mrs. Larussa hurries over to reprimand Tommy and comfort Bev.

"Look what you did, you clumsy oaf!" Bev screams. She tries to wipe her jeans with paper towels, but they're soaked.

Nancy and Taylor start giggling, which sends Bev to an even higher decibel level. "This looks like a horror movie! I don't have extra pants!"

Mrs. Larussa walks Bev out of the room to check for clothes in the Lost and Found bins in the gym. Tommy dutifully takes his seat, but he's already on to the next thing, not even registering that he just ruined someone's day.

After things calm down, I ask Mrs. Larussa if

I can use the girls' room, and she waves me off, barely looking up from Tommy, whom she now watches like a hawk. I had to start using a new bag because Craig's plastic container took up too much room in my old one, so I grab it and head down the hall.

I hear Bev in the girls' bathroom before I see her.

"I am NOT wearing this!"

I figure she's got one of her many friends in the stall with her, but when she comes out, I realize Bev is talking to herself. Even scarier, she's now wearing the same tan jumpsuit the custodians wear, but it's three sizes too big for her.

"They gave all the clothes from Lost and Found to Goodwill last week." Bev twirls around the tiled bathroom, about to cry. "My mom's got a meeting and can't pick me up till after lunch—I can't walk into the cafeteria like this!"

I almost want to give Bev a hug, but she and I aren't friends and it would probably only make her feel worse.

Then I realize there's something I *can* do.

I hurry into a stall and rummage through my bag. Craig's in his plastic container whistling while Lucinda eats a tiny bag of marshmallows.

I find the sheet of magical stickers and peel off the polka-dot dress.

whoosh! POOF! Bam!

I open the door and pretend to pull the

dress

out of my bag.

"I have this if you want to wear it." I hand her the dress, not sure what size it is or if it will even fit.

Relief washes over Bev's face and she races into the stall to try it on. She emerges with a huge smile. The dress not only fits, it looks really good.

73

"Martina, you saved me!"

It's the first time Bev has used my name and it makes me happy.

"I'll wash it and bring it back tomorrow," she says.

"It looks better on you than it ever did on me. You keep it."

She sniffs the air. "Do you smell marshmallows?"

"I don't think so," I lie.

When Bev hugs me, it's not even awkward. She thanks me again, and then holds open the door as we head back to the art room.

Bev tells the story of "Tommy the Bull in a China Shop" to everyone at lunch, going into hilarious detail about the giant jumpsuit and her new favorite polka-dot dress. She points to me when she tells the story, and at the end of the day, she invites me to sit with her on the bus.

Sticker Girl reigns supreme!

A RUFF
Afternoon

My dad's at the diner, so Eric's in charge of us until Mom gets home from work. I hate it when Eric's in charge because that means I'M the one responsible for James while Eric just sits around. Today he's hanging out with Tiffany, a girl from the next street over, so even when James unrolls the toilet paper all the way down the hall, Eric ignores him and just tries to make Tiffany laugh. Which she does. Often. A totally fake laugh that includes tossing back her hair. It's pathetic.

I follow James from room to room, coaxing

him with his toolbox, picture books, and cookies, but nothing works. I push him on the swing in the backyard, ducking underneath to pop up in front of him, which makes him yell, "Again! Again!" two dozen times. I stop him from pulling handfuls of grass by bribing him with hide-and-seek. But even that doesn't last long. He chases Lily around the yard until she gets tired too.

I drag James to the living room and ask Eric to help.

"I'd love to, but we're about to play my new game," Eric says. "Tiffany thinks she can beat me, which is hilarious."

When Tiffany gives Eric a playful shove, I want to puke on Mom's favorite rug.

"You've got it covered, Martina." Eric turns on the TV, dismissing me from the room.

After wiping up three more of James's spills, I'm out of ideas.

Until I have a great one.

My magic stickers!

If I use one of the stickers to entertain James, I'll be able to play with it too.

"Puppies or ladybug?" I ask James.

He claps his hands. "Puppies!"

For a moment, I wonder if it's a mistake to let him witness the sticker coming to life—especially after the Pegasus incident—but he's my little brother and I *do* want to share the magic with him. I open the container to give Craig some fresh air and Lucinda flies out.

"She's invading my space!" Craig says. "And she was trying to eat me!"

"I was tired and thought he'd make a good pillow." Lucinda circles around James, who squeals with delight.

"Tinker Bell!"

Lucinda screeches to a halt. "Tinker Bell is a *snob*! She thinks she's so much better than the rest of us."

"No one cares!" Craig shouts.

"Cupcake talks!" James cries.

I pray the puppies will be less work than Craig and Lucinda. I slowly peel off the sticker.

whoosh! POOF! BAM!

The adorable little **Labrador retrievers with party hats** suddenly appear in my bedroom.

And immediately begin barking.

Nonstop.

Lily wanders to the center of the Labs, sniffing each one, trying to decide if they're friend or foe. The Labs must not like being sniffed, because they bark even louder. James is laughing hysterically at the mayhem.

"Wake me up when this is over." Lucinda yawns and cuddles between the pillows on my bed.

"Me too." Craig jumps back into his plastic container.

"What's all that racket?" Eric yells from the living room. "We're trying to concentrate!"

Before I can scoop up the puppies to take them outside, James is chasing them down the hall.

"Birthday doggies!"

Lily barks loudest of all, not happy that her territory has been invaded by three rowdy party dogs. I have no idea what the history of these magical stickers is, but by the look of these pups, they've never been out in the real world before. They run, climb, jump, bark, and barrel toward the living room with James and Lily right behind.

Before I even get to hold one, Tiffany sweeps the brown puppy into her arms. "Look how cute!"

Eric tosses down the video controller and

turns to me. "Mom said one dog was enough—you're dead meat!"

I grab the yellow Lab, who's about to chew one of the legs of the coffee table.

"If you got these at the adoption center in front of the grocery store, you better bring them back," Eric continues.

"But they're adorable!" Tiffany gives my brother a wide-eyed look as she holds the puppy up to his face.

"Doggy go wee-wee," James says.

I whirl around to see the black puppy peeing on my mother's woven rug. "Noooooo!"

I pick up the pup, who continues to pee—all over my legs. "GROSS!"

James is now laughing hard.

"Let's take the doggies outside!" I grab the brown Lab to stop it from chewing the sofa cushion and shove it at James. Lily hasn't had an accident in years but she

wants in on the party and now pees on the rug too.

"Nice job, Martina," Eric says.

"*You're* supposed to be in charge, not me!"

Eric shrugs and goes back to the game. "Better take them outside or you're going to have a mess."

But Tiffany's more interested in the puppies than the video game. She asks Eric if they can sit on the grass with the dogs. Thankfully, he says yes. I stick James in his Pack 'n Play and spend the next half hour scrubbing the rug, then I clean up James and give him a snack. I wash my hands and go outside to finally play with the puppies.

Eric is sitting on the front steps on his phone.

"Where are the puppies?"

"Tiffany took them home. You can't keep them and she thought they were cute."

"Those puppies aren't yours to give!" I yell. "They're *mine*!"

"You know Mom won't let you keep three puppies. Tiffany will take good care of them." Eric holds up the game he's playing on his phone.

"Do you know if you switch around two letters in the word *Martina* you get *Martian*? I always knew you were from another planet." He laughs his stupid teenage laugh and goes back into the house.

I try to pick up Lily but she's still mad about the Labs and scampers away.

I hate Eric.

I hate James.

I hate girlfriends who dognap.

I hate babysitting.

I hate puppies.

I hate stickers.

(Okay, I take that last one back.)

A Crazy Astronomer

It's a toss-up for WORST BROTHER OF THE YEAR award. On the one hand, James lost a *Pegasus*. But Eric gave away three *puppies*! I'd give anything to be an only child right now.

On the way to Tiffany's house the next day, I practice my speech. *Hi, Tiffany—you probably don't remember me because you were so busy laughing at my brother's dumb jokes, but my name's Martina and you took my puppies! By the way, don't look at my hair. There's a fairy sleeping on my headband.*

I'm actually pretty proud of the clever place I found to hide Lucinda. And because she's asleep 99 percent of the time, she just looks like a cool hair accessory.

I can hear the dogs barking before anyone answers the door.

A woman with hair sticking up at all angles suddenly appears. Even though it's almost dinnertime, she wears a robe and slippers. News programs play on two large TV screens on the wall. "Are you here for the puppies? Take them, please! I haven't slept since they got here!"

I'm a little thrown that I won't get to do my speech but gladly take the leashes the woman offers.

"I knew my daughter wouldn't take care of these dogs," she continues. "(A) She thinks *I'll* do it. (B) She has the discipline of a nine-year-old."

I try not to take that last part personally since I AM a nine-year-old.

Behind the woman is a large telescope set up

in the middle of the living room. She sees me looking at it and nods.

"I'm an astronomer. I work at night and sleep during the day. That's why these pups are killing me."

When I tell her I'm doing a school project on constellations, she introduces herself to me as Dr. Zeidler and starts pulling books off the many shelves that line the room. The photographs of stars are amazing; she tells me to borrow as many books as I want.

Dr. Zeidler stops in her tracks. "Have you ever been to the Griffith Observatory?"

I tell her I've seen its beautiful white dome from different parts of the city but have never been inside.

"You must!" she says, and then lists off, "(A) It's one of the most important attractions in the city. (B) I work there and can give you a private tour. (C) You'll learn a lot about constellations."

She leads me to the telescope. "Let's see if we can find your favorite constellation."

I point to the bright sky outside the window. "Don't you have to look for stars at night?"

Dr. Zeidler seems disoriented, looks outside, then to her watch. "Get these puppies out so I can sleep!"

I wrangle the three puppies toward the door. "You wouldn't happen to have their party hats, would you?"

Dr. Zeidler gestures down the hall. "They're in the bathroom near the litter box."

"You have a cat, too?"

"(A) Why would someone have a litter box if they didn't have a cat? (B) I haven't seen the cat in weeks, so maybe we *don't* have one anymore, and (C) those puppies of yours didn't even know how to use a litter box."

Before I can explain that puppies don't usually *use* litter boxes, she continues.

"And (D) since they were such slow learners, I trained your pups to use the toilet instead."

"Wait—what? Puppies can't use toilets. And you trained them in a *day*?"

"It's all about setting expectations. But the yellow one has terrible aim." Dr. Zeidler shivers at the memory.

Dr. Zeidler is, hands down, the nuttiest person in the neighborhood. I thank her for the puppies, the books, and her offer to tour the observatory.

"(A) You're welcome. (B) You better get going before Tiffany comes home."

As I'm getting ready to leave, something catches my eye on the television and I ask

Dr. Zeidler if she can pause the program. My voice must sound urgent, because she does.

The news footage is from today's Dodgers game. Most people are probably watching the batter's home run, but something in the background seems familiar. I kneel close to the TV. It might be my overactive imagination but it looks like one of the clouds in the sky is pink. And shaped like a Pegasus!

I touch the screen with my finger. Could Evelyn be flying around the city? Will I ever get to see her again?

Dr. Zeidler scoots me outside, where I slip the party hats back on the dogs. (They look even cuter with them on.) If Bev, Mike, and I take Dr. Zeidler up on her offer to tour the Griffith Observatory, we'll have one of the best projects in the class.

Suddenly Lucinda buzzes around my ear. "You wouldn't happen to have any snacks, would you? I'd give anything for some popcorn right now."

I don't have time to answer, because Tiffany and a friend are riding up the street on their bikes. I do an about-face and start running with the puppies and the books, Lucinda trailing behind.

"Hey!" Tiffany shouts. "Those puppies are mine!"

"Not anymore!" I laugh as I cut through her neighbor's yard.

Doesn't Tiffany know it's not smart to mess with

An unexpected visit

Bev and Mike are excited by the prospect of doing our class presentation at the Griffith Observatory. When Mike asks me how I pulled off such a great invitation, I think about the funny story he or Bev would tell about Dr. Zeidler with the crazy hair and the puppies and the telescope. But instead, I tell them about an astronomer who lives in my neighborhood. It's a missed opportunity to get some laughs and bond with my classmates, but even with all the situations the stickers have forced me into, I still don't have the nerve to let other kids see the real me.

Ms. Graham also loves the idea of a class trip to the observatory. "What an opportunity! There's a lot of paperwork and funding involved—I'll get right on it."

"We raised money to go to the zoo last year with a bake sale," Bev says. "Can we have another one?"

"My friend Austin and I made forty dollars last weekend selling lemonade to people hiking the canyon," Mike says. "We could set up a lemonade stand too."

"Especially if people know we're trying to raise money for a class trip," Bev says.

Ms. Graham says she'll get the ball rolling and talk to our parents; Bev makes a list of all the things we'll need. I volunteer to get cups and ice from the diner.

"Your family owns a diner?" Mike asks. "That's so cool!"

Bev and Mike both wait for more details but instead of telling them about playing waitress or making up silly daily specials, I rummage through my bag as if I'm looking for something. *Why can't I share my life with potential friends?*

Unfortunately, that opens the door for Craig. "How about a party at the diner?" he says in my voice. "Maybe Sunday night?"

Bev cups her hands like a megaphone and shouts to the rest of the room. "Class party Sunday night at Martina's diner!"

"Why, that sounds like fun!" Ms. Graham says. "Am I invited too?"

I nod because I'm too baffled for words. *Did Craig just invite the whole class—including our teacher!—to the diner this weekend?* My dad offered it to us so I know he won't mind, but the reality of a party with all of my classmates has my stomach tied in knots for the rest of the day.

Bev, Mike, and I exchange addresses and phone numbers so we can iron out the details of our lemonade fund-raiser. When I get home, I hide in my room, overwhelmed by the looming party. I pull Craig out of my bag and yell at him for this recent ventriloquist stunt.

"It'll be fun!" Craig says.

To stop worrying, I make a list of all the *good* parts of having a party:

- ❤ I'll get to know my classmates better.
- ❤ It's good practice for "coming out of my shell."
- ❤ I haven't really been to any parties since we moved here.

I realize most kids would think having a party is a positive thing; maybe if I stop being so anxious, I'll think so too.

"See?" Craig points to the list in my hand. "We're going to have a good time!"

"You're not coming!" I say. "Every time you open your mouth, my life gets even more complicated!"

"You should be grateful," Craig says. "I'm helping you make friends—just like you promised your grandmother!"

Of course my abuelita will be thrilled by the

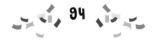

news that I'm having a party and will volunteer to help. Maybe I'm being too hard on Craig and should just go with the flow this time.

My magic fairy is sound asleep—figures!—so I decide to play with the puppies. I was expecting Mom to go nutty when she first saw them but for some—magical!—reason, she believed me when I told her I got a job dogsitting. I know she won't let me keep them but at least it bought me some time. For now, I name the puppies Blossom, Bubbles, and Buttercup after the Powerpuff Girls.

I have only three of my special stickers left so I take out some regular ones to play with instead. I find my voice balloon stickers and stick them over the voice balloons in the Garfield comic strip from Sunday's paper. I create my own story where Garfield wants something besides lasagna. But it doesn't take long for me to heed the call of my magic stickers.

I've been dying to peel off the ladybug sticker—she's *got* to be more fun than the

sleeping fairy. But after this one, there will only be two left! Should I use it now? Should I wait?

As the puppies clamber around my room, I decide to peel off the karaoke ladybug. Eric is watching TV in the family room so I close my door.

whoosh! POOF! Bam!

The Ladybug

is almost as big as Craig and is holding a shiny microphone like the one Mrs. Lajoie uses in school during assemblies. The karaoke machine looks like the one my cousin Paula has.

"You must be Martina!" the ladybug says. "I've heard so much about you."

I whip around to Craig. "I thought you stickers didn't talk to each other!"

Craig shrugs but the chatty ladybug keeps yakking. "Don't say anything to Lucinda, but she thinks you look terrible in those plaid shorts." The ladybug points to my outfit. "She's wrong— you look *great*."

I look down at my shorts. Are my stickers *gossiping* about me?

"Let's do some karaoke!" the ladybug continues. "I love to sing!"

Lucinda wakes with a start. "Is this a party? Is there food?"

I ignore my fairy, who supposedly doesn't like the way I dress, and pick up the microphone, which is now magically my size. The ladybug tells me her name is Nora and asks me what song I want to sing. Her song selection is surprisingly large and it takes me a while to choose.

"Beyoncé, good choice," Nora says.

Even though I've never done karaoke before, I find it easy to follow along with the words on Nora's screen.

Craig seems surprised I'm putting so much energy into my performance. "You're so quiet in school. How come you don't act like this with your friends?"

"She doesn't really *have* any friends," Lucinda says. "At least none that I've seen."

Nora gives me a sympathetic look that tells me she agrees. She whispers to Lucinda as if I can't hear her. "I think the puppies were happier at Tiffany's."

I hit PAUSE on the karaoke machine and turn to face my stickers. "I liked it better when stickers *didn't* talk."

"We can go back anytime," Craig says. "Is that what you want?"

I look at the cupcake, fairy, and ladybug on my bed. "I want you to stay," I finally say. "But can you try to be more *positive*?"

Nora is the first to answer. "You're right. Pick out another song and let's have some fun."

This time I choose an Elvis Presley song my dad used to sing to us when we were little. I

imitate how he used to dance, moving his hips and swooning into the microphone.

"You ain't nothing but a hound dog, crying all the time."

The stickers dance on the bed, laughing at my over-the-top singing and dramatic moves. Blossom acts like she needs to go to the bathroom, so I take her down the hall and set her on the toilet. Dr. Zeidler did a great job training them. While Blossom's in there, I keep singing, sliding down the hallway in my socks. I shout the last lines of the song and glide straight into Bev, standing in my house with a huge grin.

"Who knew quiet little Martina was a rock star? That was hilarious!"

I feel my cheeks flush and am at a loss for words.

"I wanted to drop off the list of things we need for our lemonade stand and realized you just lived two streets away. Sorry I didn't call first."

I tell her it's okay, but it's not. I'm humiliated. The whole class will probably be making fun of me tomorrow. My life is over! But when I look at Bev, she smiles.

"Don't be embarrassed," she says. "You were great!"

I get up the nerve to mumble thanks.

"Is that your puppy—going to the bathroom on a toilet?! Martina, you are *full* of surprises!"

Bev is now curious and looks into my room, where Craig, Lucinda, and Nora are all in full view, as well as Lily, Bubbles, and Buttercup in the bottom of my closet. The stickers must realize they need to behave because they all immediately go stiff, as if we're in the middle of freeze tag.

Bev scans the room, taking everything in. "You haven't eaten that cupcake yet?" she finally asks. "It must be stale by now."

I appreciate the control Craig uses not to respond to the insult.

"That ladybug is *cute*." Before I can stop her, Bev scoops Nora up in her hand. I pray Nora doesn't get chatty or gossipy.

Bev uses a baby voice, the same one my abuelita uses when she talks to Lily. "Hello, little ladybug! How are you today?"

It looks as if Nora's just about to open her mouth, so I hit PLAY on the karaoke machine. The next song in the queue is by Taylor Swift.

"I love this song!" Bev thankfully forgets about Nora and grabs the mic from my hand.

She starts singing along and when she misses some of the lyrics, she doesn't even care. I can't imagine shrugging off as many mistakes as Bev does. I look over at Craig, Lucinda, and Nora, who egg me on with their eyes. I slowly lean in toward the microphone and join Bev in the

chorus. In no time, we're searching through songs, picking out favorites, and pulling clothes out of my closet to wear as costumes.

Eric eventually sticks his head in my room to see what all the singing and laughing is about, but then just shakes his head and walks away.

This is the first friend who's come to my house since we moved here. Bev and I dance and goof around and for once I don't feel stupid or embarrassed in front of a classmate.

When Mom gets home and asks Bev if she wants to stay for dinner, she does.

And that's a first too.

Free Refills

Instead of doing research on constellations after school, Mike, Bev, and I look online for lemonade recipes. We finally opt for one that uses sugar syrup instead of solid sugar. "I hate it when the sugar just sits in the bottom of the pitcher," Bev says. "It'll be worth the extra step."

On Saturday, we get cups, ice, coolers, and napkins from Dad's diner. He's excited about the party tomorrow evening but I'm just nervous. I'm glad my abuelita will be coming to help out. I haven't seen her in a week and I miss her.

Mom stands outside the bathroom like a guard, making sure I cover myself in sunscreen since I'll be outside for most of the day.

The Angeles National Forest is a popular hiking spot on weekends; I've never been there before, but Mike is familiar with it because he bikes the canyon with his dad. His father gives us a ride and helps us unload the card table and coolers outside the trailhead. Bev made a sign with colorful striped letters and even brought a metal box for us to store our earnings. After our karaoke/dinner the other night, I find myself more comfortable around her.

It's a hot day in the canyon—already ninety degrees—and soon business is booming. With some beads from an old bracelet, I made a necklace to disguise Lucinda and Nora as cute charms. Nora's a little too big to be hanging from a chain, so she's not happy. But Lucinda's out like a light and barely notices.

Given the weather, I wanted to leave Craig at home, but he insisted on coming. As the temperature climbs, he complains about heat

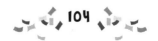

exhaustion in his plastic container, but when I take him out, he demands a parasol. Bev and Mike serve glasses of lemonade nonstop while I try to keep Craig's buttercream frosting from melting by sticking him in the cooler.

"You've got to stay on ice!" I tell Craig. "Just hang out with the lemonade!" I'm shocked when I notice we're now down to one large pitcher.

"We've made thirty-two dollars, and it's not even ten o'clock," Mike says. "We'll make enough money for a trip to the observatory."

I hold up the last pitcher and break the bad news to my classmates.

"We made *gallons.* I can't believe that's all we

have left!" Bev stares at my necklace. "It looks like those charms are moving!"

I hold the pitcher in front of my chest to block her view, but she pushes it aside.

"Hey, that's the ladybug that was in your room—how'd you make a pendant out of it?"

I mumble something about taking a craft class last summer and switch the subject back to our lemonade crisis.

Mike suggests sending his dad to the nearest store for backup; Bev thinks we should finish what we have and come back tomorrow.

Mike also stares at my necklace, then shakes his head. "I must be getting heat stroke 'cuz it looks like your charms are dancing."

Sure enough, Nora and Lucinda are restless and trying to fly off the chain. I tell Bev and Mike that I have to call my dad then run to the parking lot.

"Will you two calm down?"

"Please let us fly," Lucinda says. "We promise we'll come back before it's time to leave."

Nora looks as if she can't wait to blurt out a

secret. "We were just talking about your lemonade problem—too bad you haven't found a solution."

Both Lucinda and Nora look at me with their hands on their hips, so I finally let them off the chain. Am I missing something else?

And then it hits me.

I scramble around my bag and take out my sheet of stickers. I point to the fruity beverage. "This doesn't look like lemonade. Suppose it's a grown-up drink?"

Lucinda performs loop-de-loops around the stickers. "I guess you'll just have to see."

"But you stickers know each other. Can't you tell me what it is?"

Nora hides a smile, then sings into her mic, *"Sometimes you have to take a risk when the lemonade business is brisk."*

I know Nora and Lucinda are trying to be helpful, but I don't want to make the wrong decision. "Never mind. It looks like we wouldn't get that much anyway. Besides, I'll only have one sticker left!"

Lucinda skids to a halt an inch from my nose. "Well, I guess you know everything, don't you?"

It's ninety-something degrees, sweat is dripping down my forehead, and I'm being taunted by a fairy.

Nora points to Bev several feet away, pouring the last of the lemonade. Decisions, decisions!

I rip the sticker off the sheet.

whoosh! **POOF!** Bam!

The

pitcher

feels heavy in my hands.
"This smells *delicious*," I tell my flying friends. "What *is* it?"

"*The answer to your problem*," Nora sings. "Go!"

I hurry over to Bev and

Mike and place the pitcher on the table. I tell them my dad was in the area and dropped off some fruit punch for us to sell.

Mike pours himself a glass and takes a sip. "What is this—cherry? Raspberry? It's great." He downs the glass before I have a chance to answer.

"It's an old family recipe," I lie. "I'm not sure what's in it." Which is 100 percent true.

Bev holds up the pitcher. "We'll probably only get five or six glasses out of this, but every dollar counts." She turns to some hikers approaching the trail. "Get your ice-cold fruit punch here!"

It doesn't take long for us to have a line of thirsty hikers at the table.

"This is the best punch I've ever had!" an older woman says.

"What's in this?" a guy with a beard asks. "It's so refreshing."

I repeat the story about an old family recipe.

"It's not nice to lie to your costumers," Craig says as I reach into the cooler.

"Maybe you guys are trying to trick me. I just hope I'm doing the right thing," I say.

The older woman finishes her glass, then races up the hill in a full sprint. "Delicious!" she shouts.

Bev looks at the woman and pours herself a glass of punch. She drinks it down in a few gulps. "This stuff is *amazing*." She takes a marker from her bag and crosses out our sign. The new sign reads ENERGY DRINK—$1.

Soon we have more customers than we can handle.

Mike holds up the full pitcher. "I can't believe

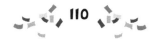

this pitcher isn't empty yet. It seems like we've sold thirty glasses."

"That *is* weird." Bev looks at the pitcher with suspicion. "Speaking of weird, why are you still carrying that cupcake around?"

I'm saved by Mike's dad, who pulls up on his bike. He grabs a glass of punch from the table, chugs it down, then wipes his mouth with the back of his arm. "How much caffeine is in this? I feel like I could ride another ten miles!"

Mike and Bev turn to me, then burst out laughing.

"We're staying till this punch runs out," Mike says.

But the punch *doesn't* run out. We stay until the three of us are too sweaty to work another minute.

Mike counts out the money at the end of the day. "We made two hundred twenty dollars— enough for *three* field trips!"

Bev holds the container up over her head and examines the bottom. "Is this a trick pitcher?"

I can't believe I'm lying to my new friend. "My dad got it at a restaurant convention. Isn't it great?"

Before Bev can ask any more questions, I grab the pitcher and pack it with the rest of my things. When I open the container, I almost don't recognize Craig, who is now a pile of chocolate goo. "Was the fund-raiser a success?" he asks.

I tell him our class will definitely be going to the observatory.

Lucinda and Nora actually gloat. *"You should listen to us more often,"* Nora sings.

Lucinda looks down at the soggy cupcake, then waves her magic wand. Craig immediately transforms into his old self.

I whip around to face her. "You *do* have fairy powers! How come you haven't used them before?"

Lucinda stretches her arms and yawns. "Too tired, I guess. By the way, this heat is brutal. I'm *exhausted*!" She fastens herself to my necklace and immediately falls asleep. Nora shrugs and does the same.

In the car on the way home, I'm the chattiest I've ever been to keep the focus off the magical punch. All three of us are excited by how amazing our constellation project will be now that we can have it at Griffith Observatory.

Bev looks at me suspiciously when she gets out of the car. "I'm going to ask your dad for that punch recipe."

I tell her no problem and that I'll see her in school on Monday.

"Did you forget about the party tomorrow night?" she asks.

I feel my stomach sink. Talking to customers today was the most people I've talked to in my entire life, and I have to do it again tomorrow with my classmates?

I need more stickers.

But I only have one left!

Diner Party!

Dad recommends setting up a taco station on the counter and serving paletas for dessert. Money's always been tight in our family so I appreciate his generosity to entertain my whole class.

The booths fill up with classmates, some I've barely spoken to before. Even a few parents have tagged along. My abuelita fusses over my classmates and knows all their names within minutes. James is excited by the new energy and runs through the diner happily screaming until Mom sticks him in the Pack 'n Play behind the counter. He wails because he's missing out on the action but stops when Bev sits next to him and hands him carrot sticks while talking in cartoon voices.

We're all surprised when Ms. Graham shows up. She has on khakis and a print shirt like she often wears to school, but she's got makeup and lipstick on and her hair is down and curly. Bev elbows me to make sure I notice; it's the kind of friend moment I used to have with Denise. It's nice to have someone at my new school to have inside jokes with too.

Ms. Graham can't believe we made over two hundred dollars at our lemonade stand yesterday. "We still have one hurdle to get over," she says. "Principal Lajoie has to sign off on the field trip, and she's a tough cookie."

"But we worked so hard!" Bev whines.

Ms. Graham tells us to keep our fingers crossed. I wonder if Lucinda can work her magic on Mrs. Lajoie the same way she used it to fix Craig yesterday.

Bev grabs Lisa and me from the booth. "Hey, let's pretend we're waitresses!"

My mom sticks her head into the group. "Martina plays that all the time—tell your friends how you play, Martina!"

I try to squelch the embarrassment growing inside me. Mom's been prompting me to "share" things with other kids since I was little and I'm horrified she's coaching me how to act in front of my classmates now.

Bev must sense my discomfort, because she immediately pretends to scribble on an invisible pad. "One order of eggs, over easy with a side of bacon."

Before Mom can butt in again, I grab a pad and pen from the counter. "Adam and Eve on a raft with a cup of mud!"

Lisa and Bev make me explain what I just ordered, then laugh when I tell them it's poached eggs on toast with coffee. They beg me to share more diner lingo, which I gladly do. Fish eyes for tapioca pudding is my favorite.

My abuelita takes a moment away from passing out juice and pulls me aside. "I'm so proud of you, Marti. I know how hard you had to work to make so many new friends."

I put my arm around her waist. "I made you a promise, right?"

She shoos me off to see if my classmates are having fun.

My dad's friend Russell makes the best ice pops on the planet and everyone has a hard time deciding which flavor to choose. (Mango-lime? Hibiscus? Coconut-papaya?) By the time everyone gathers their things to leave, all the ice pops are gone.

I thank my parents for making tonight's party a success. Neither of them says it, but I know they were worried I wouldn't make any friends this year. The relief that I finally did fueled their efforts tonight.

"What a fun evening," my abuelita says. Her

eyes sparkle; I know she was worried about me too.

Out in the parking lot, Ms. Graham looks up at the night sky. "It's so clear tonight," she says. "You hardly ever see this many stars."

I stand beside her and stare at the sky. But instead of seeing beauty, all I see is our looming constellation project. Bev, Mike, and I still have a lot of work to do.

A light startles me, and I wonder if it's a firefly. But it's Lucinda, flying off my charm bracelet and around our heads.

I can't let Ms. Graham see my magical fairy so I thank her for coming, hoping she'll leave quickly.

But something has grabbed her attention and she turns back to the sky. "Did you see that? I think it was a shooting star."

But it's Lucinda, wide awake after a long nap! She's doing cartwheels and spinning through the sky like a celestial cheerleader.

I try to distract Ms. Graham again but she's

too focused on the light swooshing through the sky.

"Stars really are something, aren't they? Your group picked a great topic."

I agree, but then also tell her we aren't sure how to bring the project to life yet. It's as if Lucinda's sparkly trail hypnotizes Ms. Graham as she counts the stars.

"Orion, Ursa Major . . . there's something magical about all of them."

It looks like Lucinda winks at me as she flies by.

"We'd be crazy not to take advantage of your contact at the observatory," Ms. Graham says.

"I'll talk to Mrs. Lajoie—tell Bev and Mike the field trip is on."

"Really?!" I notice Lucinda winding down, but I give her a sign to keep flying.

After a moment Ms. Graham looks at me and smiles. "Thanks for a lovely evening, Martina. See you tomorrow."

I wave to Ms. Graham as she drives out of the parking lot. Our project is a go! I make a mental note to confirm with Dr. Zeidler later.

Lucinda lands on my head with a thud. "Sorry," she says. "I totally misjudged that landing."

I tell her not to worry, that her light show actually helped.

"I'm so glad!" Lucinda says. "But I'm exhausted. Don't wake me up tomorrow." She wraps herself around my ponytail like an enchanted scrunchie.

As everyone gets ready to leave, I notice a few kids gathered around Lisa. She's holding her cell so everyone can watch a YouTube video.

"Doesn't that cloud look strange?" She hits PLAY again and I watch a video of a reporter covering a brush fire near the beach. Sure enough, there's a pink blur in the sky behind her.

"Evelyn!" I blurt.

Lisa corrects me. "The reporter's name is Lana, not Evelyn. But doesn't that cloud look like a Pegasus?"

I stare at the pink streak in the sky and hope my magical Pegasus is enjoying her visit to the real world—even if it's without me.

After my classmates leave, Mom comes out to load the Pack 'n Play into the car. "Tonight was fun," she says. "Maybe all those talks we had about making more of an effort paid off." She gives me a kiss on the top of my head and walks back inside.

Maybe those talks *did* help. But let's not forget the power that comes from

magical stickers.

A Sweet Idea

Ms. Graham kept her word and got the okay from our principal, who pretty much says no to everything. I was a little worried Dr. Zeidler might forget about her invitation, but when Ms. Graham calls her to discuss the details, everything's fine. She tells Ms. Graham the best time for us to come is Saturday night, probably because there won't be other schools there. Ms. Graham then sends out permission slips and handles transportation too. It's a lot more work than the other class presentations but our teacher seems as excited as we are. (Thanks, Lucinda.)

It's fun to see what the other groups have come up with for their projects. Jake, Lisa, and Tommy made a clay temple like the Incas, and Robert, Kaelyn, and Nadia made a map of our town on a giant sheet of brown paper. Because we're presenting in the evening later in the week, our project is last. Which means there's more time to prepare—and worry.

Bev, Mike, and I meet at my house to finalize the research we've been doing for weeks. Mom got tired of having the puppies scampering around the house, so Eric gave them back to Tiffany. She brought them over today just to torment me that she has them and I don't. Since her mom is giving the whole class a guided tour of the observatory, I bite my tongue and don't call her a dognapper to her face.

Mike rides back and forth in front of my house on my skateboard. "This deck is *awesome*," he says. "I usually fall off by now."

Bev and I sit on the grass and brainstorm ideas. "How about do-it-yourself constellations?" I ask. "After Dr. Zeidler lets us look through the

giant telescope, we can hand out black paper and white markers and let everyone draw their own."

"We can talk about the zodiac and astrology too," Bev says. "Have everyone read their horoscopes."

"Horoscopes are fake," Mike says as he whizzes by.

Bev notices the plastic container in my bag. "I can't believe you're still carrying around that cupcake! It must be covered in mold by now!"

Before Craig has a chance to respond, I do. "It's weird, but he's kind of my good luck charm."

"He?"

I feel my cheeks flush. "I call him Craig."

Bev collapses on the grass in laughter. "Martina Rivera, you are insane!"

It's just a normal friend moment but her laughter makes me smile, and soon I'm laughing too. Mike skateboards up the driveway and expertly hops off the board in front of us.
"Come on, you two. We've got to finish this!"

Bev suddenly springs upright. "We can bake cupcakes for the class and decorate them with constellations!"

I run inside and get one of the books I borrowed from Dr. Zeidler. "Scorpius, Orion, Perseus."

"We can make dark blue frosting with food coloring," Bev says.

"And draw the stars in yellow or white," Mike adds.

"We can use my dad's pastry bag," I say. "One of the tips is shaped like a star!"

We get to work figuring out how many we'll

need and deciding which constellations will best fit on a cupcake.

Mike holds up the papers with our notes. "We have to divide up the presentation too. Let's just each do a page since there are three of us."

The excitement comes to a screeching halt in my mind. "How about if you and Bev do the presenting while I hand out the cupcakes?"

"We have to hand the cupcakes out *after* or no one will listen to the presentation!" Bev agrees that we should each take a section.

I throw out another idea. "How about if you guys do the presentation, and I make all the cupcakes?"

"Baking is too much work for one person plus it's *fun* work. We should all do it." Bev looks at me kindly. "You know more about constellations than we do. It's not fair that Mike and I get credit for work the three of us did."

We argue for several minutes until I finally blurt out the truth. "I can't stand in front of that many people and talk. I'll be too nervous!"

Before I know it, I can barely breathe.

"Slow down," Mike says. "Take a deep breath."

"Mike and I will do the presentation if we have to," Bev finally says. "But we'll *all* bake the cupcakes, okay?"

I'm embarrassed for being so anxious about something as simple as a class project, but even spending the last few weeks surrounded by magic hasn't cured my shyness. Dented, maybe. But not cured.

The three of us make a list of what we'll need for the cupcakes; my dad's happy to help us bake them at the diner tomorrow after school. Since Bev lives only a few blocks away, she borrows my skateboard to ride home. Before she leaves, she puts her hands on my shoulders and leans in close.

"You have to conquer your fear sooner or later. You're too smart and fun to hide forever."

I've heard this from my parents, my grandmother, and my teachers my whole life. "I know," I tell her. "I'm trying."

"That's all you can do." She jumps on my board and heads down the street.

As soon as she's out of sight, Craig pops up from my bag. "I'm taking full credit for the constellation cupcake idea! You never would've thought of it without me!"

I know he's right—and I know Bev is right too. I feel bad about letting the bulk of the work fall on Mike and Bev but I'd just freeze if I have to stand in front of that many people. Craig seems to sense my anxiety and jumps into my lap and starts singing.

It's true:

CUPCaKes DO make everything better.

The Big night

The cupcakes take *way* longer than we thought to decorate, mostly because we end up eating half of them and have to bake more. We originally planned to make a different constellation for each kid in our class but end up using five of the simplest constellations. You'd need more than a cupcake for Hydra. (It takes up 3 percent of the sky.)

Since I won't be giving the presentation, I act as director when Mike and Bev rehearse. They both do a great job and I know they'll be relaxed in front of our classmates. I, on the other hand,

am nervous *for* them, which makes absolutely no sense.

Part of my anxiety comes from the fact that I have only one sticker left. After I peel off the key, am I still Sticker Girl? Does the magic go away? I don't have time to wonder about these questions because tonight's the night of our constellation project.

Since so many parents signed up to drive, Ms. Graham decided to save the bus money for another class trip. My parents insist on making a family night out of it, so Dad packs a cooler of food and tells Eric he has to come too. We get more than we bargained for when Tiffany shows up led by the three puppies on leashes. (MY puppies—whom she obviously talked her mother into keeping even though they don't let her sleep.) James squeals in his car seat as Bubbles, Buttercup, and Blossom take turns licking him on the drive to Griffith Park.

I'm shocked when we turn onto the road that leads to the observatory, because cars are lined up for miles and several people are hiking up the hill.

"Maybe there's a concert tonight," Mom suggests.

Luckily a car pulls out and Dad gets a spot in the lot so we don't have to walk far. When we finally reach the grassy lawn of the observatory, I drop my pack in amazement. The lawn is wall-to-wall with blankets and hundreds of people enjoying the city views.

I try to keep the panic out of my voice. "I thought we were getting a private tour!"

"My mom's here somewhere—you don't have to make a fuss." Tiffany rolls her eyes.

Mom sees I might lose it so she guides me to ask someone who works here where we should go. But when I spot Dr. Zeidler, I race ahead to see what's going on.

"Once a month the observatory has a free event for the public." Dr. Zeidler holds out her arms to encompass the crowd. "We call it a Star Party. (A) Because there are stars. (B) Because it's a party. Isn't it grand?"

I know it's impolite to complain but can't help it. "Tonight's our class project!"

She gives me a bewildered look, and for a minute I wonder if Lucinda and Nora have unhooked themselves from my pigtails and are flying around my head.

"Of course it is, dear! There are lots of things going on tonight, but your class will have my undivided attention!" Dr. Zeidler points to a large sign that says SUN VALLEY ELEMENTARY. "Some of your classmates have already arrived."

Mom introduces herself to Dr. Zeidler, who makes the connection that her daughter Tiffany is going out with my brother.

"Eric is such a nice young man!" she tells Mom. "His manners are impeccable!"

This, of course, is news to anyone who lives with my caveman brother, but Mom thanks

Dr. Zeidler anyway. I spot Bev and Mike and run over, with Mom trailing behind.

Mike looks around nervously. "We're not doing our presentation in front of all these people, are we?"

"Might as well share everything we learned," Bev says happily.

Ms. Graham looks as excited as Bev does. "Look at these telescopes they set up on the lawn! And it's such a clear night—I bet we'll be able to see *lots* of constellations."

Before I was worried about a few details but now I'm worried about *everything*. Where do we stand? Will our classmates be able to hear? Will there be enough cupcakes to go around? What if there's a long line for the bathroom? This last one almost throws me into panic mode so Mom accompanies Bev and me to the restroom.

Craig, as usual, senses how I feel and jumps out of my pack as Bev skips ahead and Mom answers her cell.

"You and your classmates are totally pre- pared," Craig says. "Everything will be fine."

But everything's *not* fine. Mom's now the one in panic mode. "Eric was supposed to watch James while Dad went to the car, but he can't find him. You and Bev stay here in line. I'll be right back." She runs toward our blanket, calling behind her, "Stay together and don't move!"

James has taken off lots of times, usually when Eric is supposed to be watching him. I'm not overly worried but am mad at Eric for the additional stress.

Bev takes the first empty restroom; I take the next. But when I come out, Bev is nowhere.

"Bev!" I call. "Where are you? We're supposed to stay together!"

The only response I hear is banging and screaming.

"Help!" Bev yells. "I can't get out!"

I pull on the handle of Bev's door. "Why won't it open?"

"I'm locked in!"

I tell Bev not to panic even though *I'm* panicking. I want to find Mom, but she told us to stay here. I look around. There are no staffers in sight.

Should I ask the woman next in line to help me? I remember Mom getting someone out of the diner restroom when the lock was jammed by using a bobby pin, so I rummage through my pack for a barrette that doesn't have a ladybug or a fairy on it.

A fairy!

I tug on the end of my pigtail to wake up Lucinda but she's out cold. I turn to Nora to see if she's got any bright ideas.

She holds up the mic and the karaoke machine. "It's the perfect night for 'Twinkle, Twinkle, Little Star.' How about a sing-along?"

"Sing something to wake up Lucinda! I need her!"

Craig gestures to the sheet sticking out of my wallet. "Do I have to do *everything* around here?"

Of course—the key!

I stare at the sheet. The key is my LAST MAGICAL STICKER. If I peel it off now, does that mean this adventure with my animated friends will be over? Forever?

I picture my best friend—my only friend—banging and yelling inside the locked stall.

I don't have a choice.

I peel off the sticker as fast as I can.

whoosh! POOF! Bam!

Within seconds, the

key

comes to life in my hands, which is a good thing, since Bev's still screaming.

"Hold on!" I slip the key into the lock.

It doesn't budge.

I rattle the key, turn it the other way. Still nothing.

"Martina, I'm freaking out!" Bev calls.

"I'm trying!"

Why won't the key work? Have my stickers lost their power? Did I

wait too long to use the last one? Does the key unlock something else?

Relief! I've never been so happy to see my mom, who hurries over carrying James. She finds a guard with a walkie-talkie, who calls someone over.

"Stay calm," I tell Bev through the door. "Everything's going to be fine."

When a manager finally lets Bev out, she's a wreck. My usually calm and confident friend has tears in her eyes and is coughing in spurts.

"All that shouting hurt my voice," she whispers. "How am I going to do the presentation?"

Mom puts James on her hip and searches through her purse for cough drops. I search through my bag for Lucinda. When I ask Nora and Craig where she is, they both shrug.

"She has to fix Bev's voice!"

"Lucinda's at one of the telescopes," Nora sings. "You'll have to take care of this on your own."

"I don't understand," I say. "Why didn't the key work? Why isn't Lucinda helping? Are you guys losing your magic?"

"It's not like stickers can solve *everything*," Craig answers.

He's right, of course. I shouldn't rely on magic stickers to get me through each situation that comes up. No magic key or rainbow will help me with my school project or keep these new friends when we're done. (Yes, I worry about that too.)

Bev chomps on the cough drop but still seems stressed and hoarse. "It's up to you, Martina. You have to give the presentation with Mike."

"I can't!" I'm sweating under my shirt.

By now we've caught up to the rest of the class. Ms. Graham makes a fuss over Bev but agrees we don't have a choice. I argue with our teacher, who smiles and tells me I'll do a great job.

I'm suddenly not Sticker Girl but regular old Martina who's too afraid to speak.

But this time if I fail, my friends fail with me.

And I can't let that happen.

It's time to find my *own* superpowers.

A Starry Surprise

Inside the exhibition hall, everyone in the class is amazed when Dr. Zeidler turns on the Tesla coil with its scary sparks.

After she gives us a tour of the Zeiss telescope and the planetarium, Dr. Zeidler takes out a key to one of the STAFF ONLY rooms. She jiggles it in the lock but it won't budge. "That's funny—I was going to have you do your class presentation in here. We'll have to find somewhere else."

Maybe *this* is where the key's supposed to go!

I wait till Dr. Zeidler turns around, then slip my key into the lock. It doesn't unlock the door either.

"Plan B," Dr. Zeidler says. "The rotunda."

But the rotunda is full of tourists and students studying the large pendulum marking the earth's rotation. My anxiety increases with all these false starts.

"Why am I dillydallying when we're at one of the most beautiful pieces of architecture in the city?" Dr. Zeidler swings open the large metal doors and points to the white granite steps. "You can do your presentation right here!"

Ms. Graham seats the class in neat rows, but I'm planted like a tree.

"You want us to do our project in front of all these people?" I ask.

Dr. Zeidler shrugs off my concern. "(A) People are taking pictures of the sunset. (B) They're picnicking. Don't worry so much!"

But I *do* worry. When I look across the majestic lawn, I catch a glimpse of my parents. My

abuelita and a few of her friends have joined them now too.

"Mike, Martina, why don't you begin." Ms. Graham is calm as if everything is going according to plan.

Mike looks as nervous as I am but forces himself to begin. "Martina, Bev, and I did research on constellations and we found out lots of cool things."

The three of us have rehearsed enough together for me to know this is Bev's cue. Unfortunately that now means me.

From the corner of my eye, I can see Craig, Lucinda, and Nora perched on the top of my bag. They wear the same expectant look I've seen on my mom's face. I clear my throat and begin.

"Most people think the Big Dipper is a constellation, but it's not. It's just *part* of a constellation— Ursa Major, which means 'Big Bear.'"

This is the first time in my life I've spoken in front of a large group. It may be only two sentences, but I've just cleared a massive hurdle.

"The Big Dipper is actually an *asterism*," Mike says, "which is a group of stars smaller than a constellation."

It's back to me, and this time I'm a tiny bit less nervous. "Ursa Minor is the constellation that contains the Little Dipper and Polaris—also known as the North Star. Because Polaris is one of the brightest stars in the sky and almost never moves, people have been using it to navigate for centuries."

I feel myself gaining strength as I speak. My classmates are paying attention, and even some visitors who *aren't* in our class seem to be interested. Bev sits in the front row, beaming.

Mike is about to launch into a few fun facts when our classmates—as well as the rest of the crowd—gasp. People race to adjust their telescopes while others hold up their phones to capture the most amazing celestial sight anyone has ever seen.

143

A shiny pink Pegasus gracefully soaring through the clouds.

"Evelyn!"

A few people scream as Evelyn slowly descends to the lawn of the observatory.

The crowd is silent—until Evelyn bends down right in front of me and looks me in the eye. I think she wants me to climb on. The crowd gasps again.

Bev jumps up to help me. "I have no idea what's going on, but you're not missing the chance to ride a Pegasus!"

Mom springs across the lawn, but my abuelita holds her back as I mount the flying horse.

I look down at Bev and hold out my hand. "Come on, Bev. You too."

She grins and climbs on.

"Hey, what about me?" It takes two seconds for Mike to jump on next.

Evelyn slowly takes flight, above the crowd, then above the marble domes of the observatory. I feel the breeze pass through her wings as we

soar across the lights of the city. I
hold on to her mane for dear life.

Nora and Lucinda suddenly
appear. "Isn't this fun?" Lucinda asks.

Nora tosses me her microphone, now the
perfect size for me. "You know what to do," she
adds.

"What's going on?" Bev shouts.

"Just because we're riding a Pegasus doesn't
mean we can't finish our presentation." I hand
her the mic but both she and Mike shake their
heads.

"Take it away," Mike says.

I start speaking not only to our classmates but to everyone at the observatory. "Pegasus is the seventh largest of the eighty-eight constellations. The brightest star in Pegasus is an orange supergiant at the horse's muzzle. That star is called Epsilon Pegasi and it's twelve times bigger and brighter than the sun!"

"We're riding a Pegasus!" Bev shouts.

It dawns on me that Bev no longer has a sore throat. I cover the mic and ask her if she just *pretended* to lose her voice so I'd be forced to do the presentation.

"I had to blast you out of your comfort zone," she says sheepishly.

"I'm riding on a winged horse—I think it's safe to say I'm out of my comfort zone!"

After several amazing minutes, Evelyn slowly returns to the lawn. The lights of hundreds of phones and cameras guide us to the observatory as if we're on an airport runway.

"That was the best!" Mike says. "Incredible!"

"I'm glad you enjoyed it," Evelyn says.

"WHAT?! You talk too?" Bev asks.

I should've figured Evelyn could speak since so many of the other stickers can. Evelyn nuzzles against me and closes her eyes.

"Pink horsey!" James struggles to jump out of my mom's arms as she and my dad hurry to the steps to see if I'm okay.

I'm MORE than okay. I just had the time of my life.

I spoke into a microphone.

In front of a lot of people

While in the sky.

While riding a mythological creature.

Who is pink and smells like peppermint.

That presentation deserves an A, right?

NOW the BaD NEWS

Everyone on the lawn poses for selfies with Evelyn. A news crew hurries to the steps to film but all I want to do is find Craig. He's jumping up and down on my bag, as excited as I've ever seen him.

"I'm so proud of you," Craig says. "You were confident! You were *you*."

I take that as the highest compliment. "I can't believe I did it! I wasn't even that scared."

"I'm one pleased pastry," Craig says. "I am *really* going to miss hanging out with you."

I ask him what he's talking about.

"It's time for us to go back."

"What do you mean?"

Craig looks as sincere as a cupcake can possibly look. "We go back when you don't need us anymore."

"But I *do* need you!" Tears fill my eyes. "I won't let you go! You can't."

"It's too late," Craig says. "I'm fading already."

"You're just losing crumbs." But the sadness sits inside me, unmoving. "You can't leave—you're my friend. Besides, I'm Sticker Girl!"

Craig laughs. "You'll *always* be Sticker Girl, even without magic stickers."

I grab my bag, hoping Craig is wrong about the stickers returning to the sheet. Before I can look inside, a reporter sticks a microphone in my face.

"You just rode a Pegasus! The internet is blowing up with all the videos people are posting. How do you explain what happened?"

She holds the microphone and looks at me expectantly. *What am I supposed to say?*

Thankfully Bev grabs the mic. "The three of

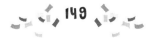

us were doing a presentation for school and thought this would be a good finale since Pegasus is a constellation. So we contacted an animatronic company in Hollywood and borrowed this Pegasus."

Mike and I look as confused as the reporter who doesn't look like she's buying Bev's story.

"We made a lot of money at our lemonade stand," Mike says.

I get into the act, telling a tall tale the way my abuelita does. "The animatronics are great. You can't see any of the wires."

The reporter excuses herself and goes to shoot some footage of Evelyn.

My abuelita slowly works her way through the crowd and puts both her hands on my cheeks. "You were wonderful! So brave!"

"Unbelievable!" my mom adds.

Eric approaches in a panic; Tiffany's crying. For a minute, I wonder if James is lost again, but he's dumping ice out of the cooler behind them. "We can't find the puppies!" Eric says. "Have you seen them?"

"Did you take them again?" Tiffany asks me. "Give them back!"

I tell her I didn't take the puppies; I don't tell her I can guess where they are. I scramble to open my bag. Sure enough, the skateboard is back on the sheet in its little slot. So is the polka-dot dress. (I'm glad Bev wasn't wearing it tonight.) The puppies and rainbow are too.

The reporter searches left, then right. "Where did that unicorn go?"

"It's a Pegasus," Bev corrects her. She's staring at the empty space where the Pegasus used to be. "Wait, your brother's puppies are missing. And the Pegasus." She pulls me aside. "Do you know what they have in common?" she whispers.

"Uhm . . . they were all here a few minutes ago?"

"Yes, but they were also on that sheet of stickers you had that day we sat together in class."

"What are you talking about? That's just a coincidence."

"Is it?" Bev asks. "All right, Martina. Come clean."

"What are you saying? That my stickers . . . came to life? That's crazy—even for someone who makes up stories like you."

But Bev will not be stopped. "Where is it?"

"Where's what?"

"That sheet of stickers." In a split second, she has grabbed my bag.

"NO!"

Before I can stop her, she's got the sheet. For someone who figured this whole thing out on her own, Bev still seems shocked. "The Pegasus. Your skateboard . . . the ladybug . . . my polka-dot dress!" She stares at me, then back at the stickers. "I knew there was something fishy about that fruit punch! How did you do this?"

"I have no idea! I've been playing with stickers my whole life, and this never happened before." I frantically snatch the sheet from Bev and collapse with relief that the cupcake slot is still empty.

She looks over my shoulder to see what I'm staring at. Of course! "I *knew* there was something strange going on with that cupcake!"

I look around the lawn, on the steps. I grab my best friend by the arm and tell her we have to find Craig.

A certain Tattoo

While we look for Craig, I fill Bev in on the sticker story, telling her about my dad and the woman with the long gray hair and the peacock tattoo who insisted he take the stickers. Bev listens patiently, as if I'm telling some normal story about a cat that followed me home from school.

We finally find Craig, who's hiding in the tray of constellation cupcakes.

I lift him into my hands. Is it my imagination or does he already feel lighter than before? "Don't go . . . please."

"Is everybody else back on the sheet?" he asks.

I stare down at my once-magical stickers. "All except you and the key."

"It's been a pleasure," he says softly.

Surprisingly Bev's jaw isn't hanging down to the ground as Craig and I have this conversation. She waits respectfully in the background, which is unlike her.

"This is Bev," I tell Craig. "She's my friend."

Craig smiles. "Sometimes one good friend is all you need. Good-bye, Martina."

Bev and I watch Craig disappear from my hand, then appear on the sheet of stickers. His large brown eyes are no longer alive but staring off into space like a flat cartoon character on a cereal box.

I can feel my cheeks burning and tears fill my eyes. "My magic stickers are gone."

Bev and I suddenly have the same idea at the same time. She watches me pull off the rainbow sticker, then the dress. But they're just regular stickers now, lifeless in my hands.

She hooks her arm through mine. "It was a great adventure though, right?"

I still feel the sting of losing Craig. But having a real flesh-and-blood best friend isn't a bad consolation prize.

I hear my little brother crying before I see him.

"Horsey go bye-bye! I want horsey!"

Mom tries to console James while Dad gathers up the blankets and cooler to take to the car. Mike hands out the cupcakes to our classmates

and Bev hugs my abuelita like a long-lost friend. Everyone gushes about how we just rode a Pegasus. My abuelita introduces Bev to her friend Juanita, whom I've known since I was little. I've never met my grandma's friend with the gray braid before; my abuelita takes me by the hand and leads me to her.

"Martina, I want you to meet Gloria. She's one of my oldest, dearest friends, and she's in town for the night."

I shake the woman's hand.

Then freeze.

A tattoo of a peacock in full plumage covers the top of her right hand. I slowly look into her eyes.

"Do you own a store? On a back road near Pomona?"

"Why, yes, I do. It's been in my family for years."

"Did you give my father some stickers for me?"

A sly smile appears on her face. "I believe I did." She turns to my abuelita, who also smiles.

"Wait," I stammer. "Did she . . . did you . . ."

Both women wait for me to finish my sentence, but the words won't come. Inside my head, however, questions explode. *Did you and my abuelita put a magic spell on those stickers? Was it to help me make friends? How did you do it? Can I please have the stickers back?* Instead, I stare at them both, shocked. Bev is also at a loss for words.

My dad scoops up James just as he's about to dump over the cooler. "Isn't it funny that your abuelita's friend is the one who gave me those stickers? It's such a small world!"

It's more than a small world—it's a crazy, incredible, *MAGICAL* world where life surprises you at every turn and all you can do is try and keep up.

unlocking something special

It's been a week since the night at the observatory, but Bev, Mike, and I still hang out after school. Bev spends a lot of time on YouTube and Facebook updating the *Pegasus Girls* blog she's been writing since our big finale with Evelyn. My stickers may have gone back to whatever magical place they came from, but our ride with Evelyn has filled Bev with an energy that's contagious.

We plan lots of fun projects for the summer and start a Sticker Girl club after school where kids bring their own stickers to trade. (We even let boys in.) The attention and fuss after our flight makes me uncomfortable sometimes but it's exciting too.

There's one thing I *haven't* found energy for. Ever since my magic stickers went back to the sheet, I haven't looked at them. The thought of staring at Craig's blank face keeps me from enjoying him and the others as regular stickers. I hate to admit it, but I bought dozens of cupcake stickers this month, hoping one of them would come to life. None of them have.

"How did you remember what stickers I had on that sheet?" I ask Bev. "You only saw them that one day."

"I told you before that I have a great visual memory, and I love stickers, so it was easy. Speaking of which, can I *please* see them?"

She has asked me many times since the presentation but I always say no.

"You need to move on, Sticker Girl," Bev says. "You'll never get your superpowers back dreaming about the past."

She's right, of course. Daydreaming about Evelyn or Craig won't make them come back to life. I know that.

"Let's play with them like they're *ordinary* stickers," Bev suggests. "Let's stick them all over our sneakers." She moves her eyebrows up and down, waiting for my answer.

"Okay," I answer. "Let me find them."

"As if you don't know where they are," Bev teases.

For someone who's only been my best friend for a few weeks, Bev already knows me pretty well. I go to the top of my closet and take out the stickers.

We both stare at the sheet in shock.

The key never went back into its slot.

"Where's the real key?" Bev shouts. "Do you remember where you put it? When did you have it last?"

"At the observatory—trying to get you out of the bathroom, then Dr. Zeidler's office!" I dump out my bag, and look through the top drawer of

my desk and the little box I keep my bracelets in. But the magic key is nowhere to be found.

"Think!" Bev says. "Maybe it can bring the other stickers back to life!"

I hate to burst Bev's bubble but I know in my heart those stickers did what they came to do and won't be returning.

Bev and I empty my dresser, then my closet.

"Aha!" Bev holds up the key. "It was inside one of your shoes." She points to the hangers above us. "Probably fell out of the pocket of what you wore that night."

We race through the house, trying the key on every door. We try it on the rolltop desk my dad uses in the garage but that doesn't work either.

As we go room by room, questions ricochet inside my head. *Why would the key stay behind? Has it been trying to get back this whole time like the alien in* E.T.? *Does it unlock a treasure chest that will make me rich?*

"Call your grandmother," Bev says. "If she and her friend actually put a spell on those stickers, she'll know what to do."

"My abuelita still hasn't admitted she had anything to do with the stickers. Every time I ask, she just smiles."

Bev nods. "That means she's guilty. You need to call her."

If my abuelita was behind the magical stickers as a way to lure me out of my shell, she certainly deserves a parade. Each sticker got me one step closer to the new me. I also know the last thing my abuelita would want is for me to ask for help. If the key getting left behind is some kind of puzzle, she'd want me to solve it myself.

"Let's start from the beginning," I tell Bev.

We grab chocolate chip cookies from the kitchen and jump onto the couch. I tell Bev—for the millionth time—about my father coming home with presents for all of us after the restaurant convention.

"Details," Bev says. "Give me details."

I tell her how my mom came in with bags of groceries, how Eric was so happy with his new cell phone case. "Dad got James a toy toolbox and me those stickers."

163

"Did he get them at the same store?"

I take another cookie from the bag and think. "I'm not sure, but I think so."

Before I can put the cookie in my mouth, Bev grabs it out of my hand.

"The toolbox!" we both scream.

We run down the hall to the room James shares with Eric. Between Eric's clothes and James's toys, we can barely see the floor.

The frantic search begins.

We find blocks and books and soldiers and balls and stuffed animals, but we can't find the toolbox. After several frustrating minutes, I finally spot the red plastic box underneath James's crib.

Carefully, I slide it out and place it in front of Bev.

"My brother's used this a zillion times but I've never seen him lock it."

Bev tests the cover. "Well, it's locked now."

I slowly insert the key.

It fits!

Before lifting the cover, I pause. "Whatever we find in here, we split fifty-fifty."

"No way," Bev laughs. "Whatever's in there is yours. I'm just along for the ride."

"Even if it's a million dollars?"

"A million dollars wouldn't fit in that box." Bev smiles. "Besides, *you're* Sticker Girl, not me."

What I want to find most in this toy toolbox isn't a million dollars but a grumpy little cupcake named Craig.

I lift the cover and take out the plastic wrench, screwdriver, hammer, and bolt. Bev reaches in and takes out the yellow saw.

We stare into the empty toolbox.

"But the key opened it," Bev says.

I hold up the hammer and screwdriver. "Are we supposed to use these tools to build something? Melt them down into another key?" We bat around ideas until we can't think of any more.

I gather up the tools and dump them back in

the toolbox. "I guess the key just got left behind and that's the end of it."

But as I toss the tools into the box, a sliver of paper catches my eye. I dump out the tools again and run my hand along the inside cover.

"There's something stuck to the top of the case!"

"Get it out, get it out!" Bev shouts.

I slowly pull out a sparkly sheet of stickers.

Bev looks at the sheet, then at me. "Do you think they're . . ."

"Magic? There's only one way to find out." We scan the sheet together. The stickers are shiny and new and I've never seen any of them before.

Except for one—

a smirking chocolate cupcake!

GOFISH

JANET TASHJIAN

What did you want to be when you grew up?
When I was really young, I used to make a lot of
clothes for my dolls out of felt. Back then, I thought
about being a fashion designer.

**What's your most embarrassing childhood
memory?**
Having my shoe come off onstage during a school
recital.

What's your favorite childhood memory?
Being outside in summer, at the end of the day when
the light changes. It's still my favorite time of day.

What was your favorite thing about school?
When the bell rang at three o'clock.

**What was your least favorite thing about
school?**
The school uniforms didn't have pockets.

 SQUARE FISH

What were your hobbies as a kid? What are your hobbies now?

I used to sew a lot. I sew less now, but I still like to work with my hands.

What was your first job, and what was your "worst" job?

I did a lot of babysitting, of course, and waitressing. I also worked on an assembly line when I was sixteen—it wasn't as much fun as it looked on *I Love Lucy*.

How did you celebrate publishing your first book?

I did a book signing near my home town, and my tenth-grade English teacher came. I hadn't seen her since high school; it was a real treat.

Where do you write your books?

At my house in LA, often sitting outside. The benefit of writing in longhand is that I can write anywhere, so I also go to coffee shops and restaurants to get out of the house.

What sparked your inspiration for *Sticker Girl*?

I start all of my books by asking the question "What if?". My editor, Christy Ottaviano, has always put stickers on every letter and memo she's sent me for the past twenty years. And I know so many little girls who are obsessed with stickers, too. So I thought: *What if a little girl had a sheet of stickers that came to life?* Would she be thrilled or would they cause trouble for her? I had so much fun making up scenarios for Martina, and Christy immediately loved the idea.

Did you collect stickers as a kid? Do you collect them now?
I wasn't really a sticker kid but I did love Colorforms. I realize I'm dating myself with the reference, but I used to love creating scenes with the colorful plastic stickers (I still have a felt board too!). I did always cut things out of paper, felt and fabric, and I still love making collages; I just got some vintage paper dolls at a yard sale that I'll do something with. So even though I don't buy a lot of stickers, I kind of make my own.

If you could magically bring one of your belongings to life, which would it be? Why?
OMG—this is a tough one! I have piles of vintage fabric that I love but wouldn't be that much fun alive. I also have a TON of board games but I'm not sure how much fun they'd be either. I *do* have a lot of doll heads—they actually might be cool to bring to life. They'd probably complain about being stuck in a giant glass jar in my living room but they might also have some interesting things to say. Wait, what am I talking about—I have a unicorn raft in my pool! That's the one!

Were you shy as a kid, like Martina?
I was pretty quiet as a kid; I was definitely a bookworm. I blossomed into a chatterbox as I got older. I am definitely not shy now.

Martina and Bev become close friends. What is your favorite thing to do with a close friend?

I love playing strategy games; I love hiking; I love going out to dinner. But my favorite thing to do with a BFF is to swim in my pool and make up stories. Most of my friends are creative and love to exercise their imaginations too. Making up stories for your own amusement is awesome; doing it with a friend is even better.

Of the books you've written, which is your favorite?

I love *Tru Confessions* because it was my first. I love *The Gospel According to Larry* because I really accomplished what I set out to do. I love *My Life as a Book* because I got to work with my son. There's something special about all my books.

What challenges do you face in the writing process, and how do you overcome them?

Writing books is a marathon and my personality is more like a sprinter's. I have to work very hard to stay on task. So I write every day with a clear goal of how much I need to get done.

Which of your characters is most like you?

There's a lot of me in Larry, for sure. I also relate to the mother in *My Life as a Book*. Trudy's ambition in *Tru Confessions* is also very me.

What makes you laugh out loud?
My son. He's hilarious—makes me laugh out loud every day.

What do you do on a rainy day?
In LA, you don't get a lot of rainy days, so when it does rain, it's a great excuse to sit on the couch and watch movies.

What's your idea of fun?
Hanging out with friends, going to movies, discovering new places in the city, walking my dog on the bluff.

What's your favorite song?
I could never come up with just one favorite song. I love music and listen to it all day long. One song I could never live without is Frank Zappa's "Peaches en Regalia." It makes me smile every time I hear it.

Who is your favorite fictional character?
It would be impossible to choose.

What was your favorite book when you were a kid? Do you have a favorite book now?
I used to read a lot of Nancy Drew and Encyclopedia Brown books. When I got older, it was Kurt Vonnegut. I read a lot of nonfiction now, too.

What's your favorite TV show or movie?
I like *Modern Family* and *Glee*. My favorite movie of all time is *Chinatown*.

 SQUARE FISH

If you were stranded on a desert island, who would you want for company?

My husband, my son, and my dog—I couldn't imagine being there without them. I could stay on a desert island forever if they were there with me.

If you could travel anywhere in the world, where would you go and what would you do?

I've done a lot of traveling but have never been to South America, so I guess that would be next.

What's the best advice you ever received about writing?

Hemingway's advice that the most important thing about a first draft is to finish it. I live by that rule.

Do you ever get writer's block? What do you do to get back on track?

I hardly ever get writer's block; I have the opposite problem—so many stories rattle around in my mind that I have to constantly stay on task to finish one project without getting distracted by another one. But when I do get stuck, I use another Hemingway trick. He said to start by writing one true sentence about your character. Then another, then another. You dig yourself out of the hole of writer's block one sentence at a time.

What do you want readers to remember about your books?

That I had fun writing them.

What would you do if you ever stopped writing?
Sit on a beach and make up stories for my own amusement. Or if I were starting a new career from scratch, I'd study architecture.

What do you like best about yourself?
I have a big, loud laugh.

What do you consider to be your greatest accomplishment?
Raising a smart, empathetic, funny son.

What do you wish you could do better?
Exercise—I'm horrible and unmotivated!

What would your readers be most surprised to learn about you?
I'm a huge Three Stooges fan—I'm watching them now as I write this!

SQUARE FISH

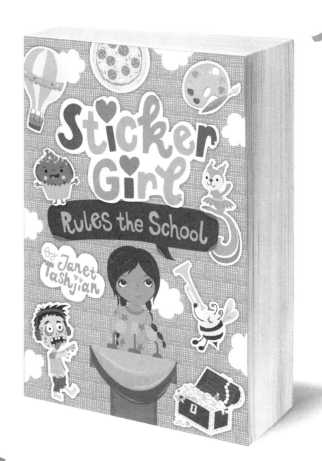

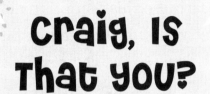

CRAIG, IS THAT YOU?

You know how sometimes even the most patient kid practically crawls out of her skin with anticipation? Well, seeing Craig—my funny, grumpy cupcake friend—on the new sheet of stickers gives me that feeling.

I take a deep breath and count to ten.

My friend Bev looks over my shoulder at the sheet of stickers. I'm sure she's thinking the same thing: will *these* stickers be magical too?

"Let me guess. You're trying to decide if you should peel off Craig first, right?" Bev says.

"Especially since one of the *other* stickers is a treasure chest."

To be honest, it's not a tough decision. Even though Craig caused his share of trouble last time, he was pretty fun to have around. But there are only ten stickers, so pacing myself is a must.

Besides Craig, the new stickers are a . . .

♥ girl soccer player

♥chipmunk
 ballerina

♥ honeybee with
 a trumpet

● treasure chest

● pizza

● cell phone

● zombie DJ

● palette with paint

● hot-air balloon

I just hope this new batch of stickers turns out to be a little less trouble than the last sheet.

"I can't believe you're hesitating," Bev jokes. "You have to use at least ONE while I'm here."

It's not that I don't want to share the magic with Bev—I mean, she rode with me on a Pegasus that was once a sticker. But what if something goes wrong? What if the stickers we just found hidden in my little brother's toy toolbox aren't enchanted like the last batch? Or worse—what if they're evil?

Bev sits down on my bed. "If you don't hurry up and do it, I will," she teases.

She's right. Why am I hesitating? I gently peel my little cupcake friend off the sheet of stickers.

whoosh! poof! Bam!

Craig immediately appears in my hand, coughing and wheezing.

"Martina! I missed you!"

When Bev whips her head around to see him, I can't help but smile.

This is real.

This is happening.

my stickers are alive— again!

A POUtY BaKed good

Since you can't really hug a cupcake, it's a bit awkward showing Craig how happy I am to see him. The last thing I want to do is squish him on his first day back. He remembers Bev and says hello.

There are a million questions I want to ask: Where did he go when the stickers returned to the sheet? Was it like sleeping or being dead? Is there anything he should warn me about BEFORE I peel the stickers off this time? (I may decide to take a pass on the zombie. . . .)

It's as if Craig can read my mind, because he crosses his arms and scowls. "I'm not even here for a minute and you're already wondering what we stickers can do for you! Ever think about what WE might want out of this, Martina? We're the ones who finally get to come alive—you should take OUR needs into consideration. It's just plain DULL sitting on that sheet, waiting to get peeled off!"

Bev claps her hand over her mouth and tries not to laugh.

"He's very opinionated," I say.

As Craig stomps around my desk, tiny crumbs fly off him. I tell him if he doesn't stop getting so upset, he'll be a *mini* cupcake by the end of the day.

"Just keep those monsters away from me."

I don't know what he's talking about until I see my brother James and my dog, Lily, in the hall. James is only two years old and Lily's a Chihuahua, so neither can be categorized as a monster, but I suppose if Craig tastes as good as he looks, everyone's a potential threat.

"Cupcake!" James squeals. "Cupcake talks!"

Lily arches her back and lets out a low growl, so Bev picks her up and rubs her belly. "I can't believe you chose Craig first! Ninety-nine percent of the people in the universe would've taken the treasure chest."

Maybe Bev's right and I'm being too cautious with my magical stickers. Maybe since I've got a friend to hang out with now, their magic will be much more manageable.

I try to hand the sheet of stickers to Bev but she shakes her head. "No way. They probably only work when *you* peel them off."

"There's one way to find out." I continue holding the sheet of stickers out to her.

"I don't think that's such a good idea," Craig says. "There's no telling what will happen if you let everyone in the world share in the magic."

Considering I pretty much have only one or two friends here, Craig's warning is definitely overkill. But his comment does make me realize it might not be smart to tempt fate.

"You're right, Bev—let's peel off the treasure chest." Both of us hover over the sticker as I lift it off the sheet.

whoosh! Poof! Bam!

A chest

overflowing with gold, diamonds, rubies, and emeralds is now in the center of my room. Bev and I stare at the old wooden trunk like a couple of pirates.

Then we scream.

Craig laughs. "It's like you two have never seen a fortune before."

"Probably because we HAVEN'T!" Bev takes

a handful of diamonds and rubies and examines them.

I think about all the coupons my mom cuts out, how many clothes she mends, how many hours my father works at the diner he owns. Suddenly we're rich! This can really change our lives!

Lily sniffs at the gems scattered on the rug while James dives into the chest.

How am I going to explain this windfall to my parents? How are we going to move this trunk? How can I hide this from my brother Eric, who thinks what's mine is his just because he's older?

But most important—WHAT AM I GOING TO DO WITH ALL THESE JEWELS?

Don't miss the My Life series, also by Janet Tashjian!

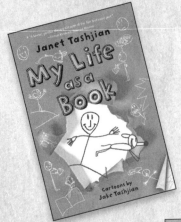

★ "A kinder, gentler Wimpy Kid with all the fun and more plot."
—*KIRKUS REVIEWS*, STARRED REVIEW

★ "Give this to kids who think they don't like reading. It might change their minds." —*BOOKLIST*, STARRED REVIEW

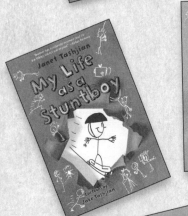

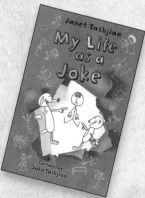